ALLIANCE WITH THE ALIEN PIRATE

THE CURSED COMPOUND
BOOK ONE

IVY KNOX

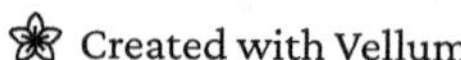 Created with Vellum

AUTHOR'S NOTE

If you don't have any concerns regarding content and how it may affect you, **feel free to skip ahead to avoid spoilers**!

This book contains scenes that reference kidnapping, psychological and physical torture, substance abuse, drug overdose, parental death, cancer, racism, sexism, as well as graphic violence which may be triggering for some. If you or someone you know is in need of support, there are places you can go for help. I have listed some resources at the end of this book.

Alliance with the Alien Pirate was originally published in *Supra Velum: A Spooky Sci-fi Romance Anthology*. This version has additional chapters, more steamy scenes, and a preview of book two in The Cursed Compound series. Enjoy!

PROLOGUE

ERIN

In the back of a cramped spaceship with twenty-three other women, I'm the only one who isn't crying. We've all been kidnapped from Earth, and what lies ahead for us is completely unknown. We could be on the way to being sold off as sex slaves to creatures with ten legs and venomous spikes covering their pocket rockets.

I like to think we've been selected to live out our remaining years in a castle on an unknown planet, with our days spent being fed grapes and fanned with palm fronds by aliens who look like Ryan Gosling, but I'm an optimist.

The heaving sobs all around me tell me that none of these women share my hopes for the future.

I haven't shed a single tear since I was taken. Maybe it's because it's hotter than the devil's armpit in here, and I know that crying will make me sweat even more, or maybe it's because I've already shed a lifetime of tears, and my tear ducts have run dry. I don't know.

What I do know, is that a) this shapeless sack we're forced to wear is giving me the itchiest wedgie in history, and b) things can only get better.

For a second, I consider if this line of thinking is naïve. If I were to say it out loud, I'm certain the women sitting on either side of me atop this creaky wooden bench would say yes. But they don't know what I've lived through.

They don't know that I was twelve when I found my mother's dead body the morning after she overdosed, or that I was in the room when my sister let out her final breath after a long battle with cancer, or that I watched Granny have a heart attack in the kitchen and collapse with a bowl of muffin batter clutched in her hands. Even my cat, Shrimp, passed away after a brief illness at the young age of three.

There was no one left for me to love back on Earth before I was taken. Death had claimed them all, and right before my eyes.

When you get used to death the way I was, there's not much left to fear. I was scared when I woke up naked inside a dirty metal cage in the back of a spaceship, sure, but instead of crying, I was curious. Was it my turn to die? Would the kidnappers off me in a creative way, at least? Would I be thrown out of the spaceship to die in the darkness that filled deep space? Would I be tortured first? Or would one of our slimy, tentacled alien guards slit my throat with a rusty dagger?

None of that has happened. Instead, I was stripped bare of the clothes I was wearing when I was taken, which was a blue-checkered pair of men's boxers and an oversized t-shirt I bought at Goodwill, since I was asleep at the time. Then, I, along with the other women, were shoved into a large shower where the guards scrubbed our skin with a liquid soap that smelled like fresh mulch and an abrasive sponge that left our skin red and raw. We were given these large, black sacks that feel like they're made from burlap and wool, with matching black slippers that barely have enough tread to protect the bottoms of our feet from the mysterious wetness that covers the floor.

That was two days ago, I think. It's hard to tell in here since there aren't any windows or clocks.

Since then, the ship has made several stops. The first one was a pickup, where six more women joined us, and the rest have been drop-offs. To where, I have no idea, but I'd bet my behind that the surroundings will be more pleasant than this.

I've spent so much time at rock bottom, I've added throw pillows to that jagged pile of rocks. Heck, I've even put up wallpaper and pondered how else to decorate the space. That's how intimately I know pain and loss, and there's comfort in that, because what could these creatures do to really rattle me at this point? Not much.

I let out a sigh as I wipe the sweat from my forehead, and the woman next to me furrows her brow. "Why aren't you afraid?" she asks through loud sniffles.

I reply with a shrug. I take in her long, blonde hair, which was smooth and wavy two days ago and is now limp and oily. She wears a slim gold band on her ring finger, and I spot a tattoo on her wrist of two birthdates stacked on top of each other. The top one is about five years ago, the bottom about three. Her children, I assume. Of course she's scared. She's lost so much, and I doubt she'll get to see her family ever again.

What an honor it is to be missed, and to have people to miss in return. I wish I knew what that felt like.

"Do you know where we're headed?" she asks.

I shake my head.

Her shoulders shake with the force of her sobs, as if me reminding her that our destination is unknown has confirmed her worse fears. Guilt washes over me, and I take her hand in mine. "It'll be okay though," I promise her.

"How do you know? What if it's worse?" She wipes the snot from her nose. "We're going to die. They're going to kill us."

I take her hand in my lap and give her a reassuring squeeze. "Darlin', it's not gonna be worse. Look around," I say, sweeping my arm through the air and gesturing to the bucket in the corner that we have to share to relieve ourselves. "Whatever our final destination is, it has to be better than this."

It *has* to.

CHAPTER 1

ERIN

SIX MONTHS LATER...

Instead of a bucket to do my business in, I've got a fully functioning space toilet. I also have a place to shower, clothes that don't irritate my skin, boots that protect my feet, and my very own bed. Granted, life on Station N87 isn't a cakewalk, and I've yet to encounter anyone who remotely resembles Ryan Gosling.

I've also been given strict orders from my boss to not linger in the corridors or by the market before and after my shifts at The Meat Pocket, but just as I suspected, things *are* better than they were on the ship that brought me here.

I step onto the freight elevator and take it three floors up to the restaurant. This elevator is mere steps from The Meat Pocket's back entrance, so it's the safest one to use for my short commute. I wave to my boss, L'Uvin Soa, as I enter. He replies with his usual surly grunt as I pass him, then returns his attention to the puzzle on the table in front of him. I greet every coworker I pass as I throw on my hairnet, my apron, and my gloves and make my way to the fryer. L'Uvin Soa is not the friendliest boss I've ever had. Heck, he wouldn't even make the top ten, but he does look out for me.

The day I was dropped off here in my itchy sack, he was waiting at the port. He took me by the arm, albeit somewhat roughly, but when I winced in pain, he loosened his grip. He hissed at anyone who made lewd comments as I passed, and he gave me a place to live, clothing, and a job. He also took the time to teach me basic Crindan, which is the universal language of this galaxy, and gifted me hundreds of digital files to continue my language studies.

"Any pending orders I need to start?" I ask Gr'va, my coworker and roommate, in Crindan.

"No, we are on pace," she replies as she lifts clean dishes from the sink into their respective buckets and starts spraying the dirty ones with water.

"Jolly day, Erin," Haibomoo, the two-foot-tall male with three arms who chops all the veggies, says as he puts three containers of chopped leaves into the chiller.

"Jolly day, Haibomoo," I say back with a warm smile.

It's a strange greeting, but I've gotten used to it over time.

The tablet on the shelf above the fryer beeps twice, indicating a new order has been placed, and I open the chiller to grab a handful of *kaoliu* meat before dropping it on the fryer. Using my flat-edged tongs, I push the meat around, creating a thin, even layer before throwing some root vegetables on top.

Working the fryer isn't a glamorous job, but I like how it never changes. I do the same thing every day, and L'Uvin Soa pays me a few credits each month for the hours I put in. As his employees, Gr'va and I don't have to pay rent, and we usually take home enough food from the restaurant to keep us fed between shifts, so the credits we earn are ours to keep. I'm saving mine, and, hopefully, one day I'll have enough to buy my way off the station and get a house on a nearby planet that welcomes my kind.

"Anything exciting happen this mornin'?" I ask Gr'va once I finish stuffing our signature fried bread with the meat and veggies and pass the plate to the server shelf, indicating it's done.

"A fight broke out at the brothel upstairs when I arrived. I could hear shots being fired above us," she explains.

I chuckle under my breath. "Yikes, another one?"

There's always drama at the brothel. I've learned that gun fights are a weekly occurrence up there. Luckily, it's rare that the fighting spreads to our floor. Unless the Thorn Thackers show up—a gang of nine-foot-tall, porcupine-looking fellas who seek to cause chaos wherever they go. They eat here, drink too much at the tavern three doors down, and fight, steal, kidnap, and kill. Their MO is pure destruction.

A few days after I arrived, they got into a tussle with someone in the corridor just beyond the restaurant's front doors as I was leaving for the day. I quickly found myself trapped between them and a rival gang who were seconds away from being filled with bacteria-coated bullets. L'Uvin Soa saw me and yanked me back inside just in time. That rival gang died screaming in pain, and since then, I've heeded L'Uvin Soa's warning to never linger outside the restaurant again.

"Your skin is not thick enough, and your bones are like twigs," he said that day. "Unsupervised humans are not safe here."

These stations, he explained, are violent, lawless pit stops for the shadiest characters in space. It's not worth the risk to wander about. L'Uvin Soa keeps his weakest staffers in the kitchen, where we can remain hidden, and the tougher crea-tures working on the floor. He has an impenetrable shell that covers his back, and a few of the servers do too. The other servers are all *finzars*, a species with owl-like heads that spin all the way around and kangaroo bodies with extremely thick hides.

They can handle themselves in a fight, whereas me and Haibomoo stay in the kitchen at all times.

Gr'va is the only exception to this rule. Her pretty purple scales are several inches thick and could likely protect her from serious injury in a gun fight, but L'Uvin Soa keeps her in the kitchen because her manners are atrocious. She's rude to customers, and on more than one occasion has taken food off their plates as she was serving it, so she spends most of her work hours washing dishes. If she sneaks food scraps at the sink, at least the customers can't see her.

When the lunch rush hits, Haibomoo takes a step stool and joins me on the fryer. We work quickly to prepare all the orders that come in. His shift ends not long after that, as does Gr'va's, and the lull between lunch and dinner has me lost in thought as I scrape the burned meat scraps off the edges and toss them into a bucket at my feet.

I can't help but feel that my life is missing something. Something, I don't know, bigger than this. I'm grateful to be alive, and to have a safe place to sleep, but I have very little freedom here. We don't have a TV or books to read, other than textbooks on the Crindan language, so anytime I'm not asleep, I'm basically staring at my bedroom wall counting the cracks in the paint.

Station N87 is either as boring as a PowerPoint presentation on the history of Manila folders, or it's like the Wild Wild West, wherein I'm neither the hero nor the villain. I'm more like the empty beer bottle on the countertop of the saloon that's seconds away from being hit with a bullet and shattering into a million pieces.

I could probably stay here forever if I wanted to. L'Uvin Soa has said as much. He's always looking for more help. I'm just not sure my sanity would remain intact if I did.

What I need is stability and safety. Lord knows I didn't have a lick of either growing up. Mom did the best she could, I think, despite her demons. But safety is severely lacking here.

If I've got nothing to cling to but my daily routines, I should at least be able to go about them without the risk of getting murdered by port hooligans.

Lately, I've been fantasizing about a little cottage in the middle of a field, no neighbors in sight, and a garden on the side of the house where I can grow fresh flowers and vegetables. It'd be so nice to have a place that's entirely mine, with a porch and rocking chair from which I can watch the sunset while drinking lemonade. I don't need a mansion, or even the hunky Gosling-esque servants feeding me grapes. A place that's bigger than the closet I currently reside in sure would be nice though.

Granny would say, "Life doesn't owe you squat, girl. You want your situation to change? You best pull up your bootstraps and get to work."

But how much work will it take to achieve a life that a lot of people would never be happy settling for? Most would consider living alone in a one- or two-bedroom house in the middle of a field a lonely, sad existence, not a dream. That's all I want though. If there was some way to achieve that, I'd give anything.

"What are y'all looking at?" I ask two of the servers as I toss my apron and hairnet into my assigned cubby. There's no Crindan word for "y'all," but they've gotten used to me butchering the language with my Southern accent and weird slang. Their eyes are glued to the tablet above the employee resources bulletin board by the back door. Oov and Tixuq quietly mutter something to each other, then Oov turns to me and says, "There is an offer to join a research study on Huva II."

"Research study?" I reply, my interest piqued. Huva II isn't that far, and I've heard there are shuttles that go back and forth from the station every day.

I step between them and watch as the advertisement begins to replay.

"Are you looking for a new beginning on a planet in the Crinda Galaxy but have no credits to your name?" the beautiful alien woman with glimmering green scales says in a jovial tone. "Come to the Cursed Compound on Huva II and participate in our brand-new interactive research study."

The camera flies past her head and zooms in on a tall, ominous-looking white castle behind her. Red fog rises from the towers, sending chills down my spine. There are muffled screams, growls, and loud roars coming from the building, and the footage shifts to an inside look at the castle, where a massive beast with black fur and red fangs chases a clearly frightened, stout, gray-feathered female through a dimly lit hallway.

I gasp with delight. "A haunted house?" I ask Tixuq, grabbing his wrist and bouncing on the balls of my feet. "Is that what this is?"

He gives me a blank look. "I do not know what that is."

My heart breaks for him. What a spectacular experience to miss out on. "You know, a place where people go to be scared and get chased by monsters?"

Oov grunts and raises a plated brow. "Why would anyone seek that out?"

"Because it's fun," I say, just as the woman on the ad continues speaking.

"There are no restrictions on who can apply, and the only requirement is to complete the course. Those who do will receive two-hundred-thousand credits upon reaching the finish line."

My jaw falls open.

All I have to do is make my way through a haunted house and I get two-hundred-thousand credits? Easy-peasy lemon squeezy.

This is it. This is my way out.

CHAPTER 2

ERIN

Everyone on the shuttle to Huva II is staring at me, and I wonder if it's because I'm the only human on board or if it's because I reek. Working as a fry cook keeps a roof over my head, but it also means the smell of meat and oil clings to my hair and emanates from my every pore, no matter how many times I shower.

Oh well. I might be hanging out like a hair on a biscuit, but I don't have time to stress over it. I need to focus on what lies ahead, and that's the research study I signed up for. All I need to do is make it through the entire compound in order to be eligible for the big payout. It'll be more than enough to quit my job and buy a house on the neighboring planet, Yeronix. Humans are welcome there, which is a rarity in space.

My watch buzzes, and a photo of Gr'va pops up on the screen.

"It's only been four hours since I left, Gr'va," I say with a smile. "You miss me that much already?"

Her feathered brow furrows, and she blinks several times before she speaks. "Not at all," she says. "I'll be eating the slice of *bunti piz* cake you left in the chiller." She lifts the cake into the frame to show me, then takes a large bite, the gray frosting sticking to the corners of her mouth. "That's what you wanted me to do, yes? Tell you before I eat your food?"

"Pretty sure I wanted you to *ask* first," I gently correct her, "but it's fine. I won't be back for a few days, at least, so it would've gone bad anyway. Enjoy." That is, if I go back at all. If I make it through the study and get my credits, I plan on going straight to Yeronix to set up shop. I didn't leave anything of value at the station anyway.

"A few days?" she scoffs with her mouth full. "It's unlikely you will survive. I have already moved your mattress into my room since you won't be coming back."

Gr'va couldn't keep a roommate for more than a month before I came along. I suspect it's because she has the manners of a wild boar. She has never, not once, chewed with her mouth closed, she steals my stuff, and she never closes the bathroom door when she uses her strange litter box. I have no idea if it's a cultural thing among the lavender-scaled beings from her home planet or if that's just her personality. Most of the time, I appreciate her loud way of existing. But today, what I need is encouragement.

"I know what everyone says about Huva II, but I promise you, I've got this," I reassure her. "Like I said before, it's just a big, haunted house, and I love those. Before I was taken from Earth, I'd spend the weekends in autumn hitting every haunted house and hayride I could find. It'll be easy."

"It will *not* be easy," she insists, her mouth forming a grim line beneath her black beak. "Huva II is a chaotic cesspool of a planet where Empress Motavvi and her kin have tortured entire species for the sake of their research. The prize she offers at the end of this Cursed Compound study won't be worth it, and you might not even live to collect it."

"So what am I supposed to do? Spend the rest of my life

working at The Meat Pocket, barely scraping by on the few credits we earn each month?" I ask her. "I want a home and a garden that I can plant myself. Besides, the station isn't safe for humans, Gr'va, and I'm tired of hiding in our apartment whenever I'm not working. I go to bed each night thankful I survived another day. I just want a safe, quiet life."

Gr'va laughs, throwing her head back as little cake crumbs spray out of her mouth and across the screen. "You think Empress Motavvi is the key to your eternal happiness? I care not what the advertisement said. With the empress, there is always more to what she offers. A trick of some kind."

I understand her pessimism. Like me, she was kidnapped from her home planet and has struggled to survive ever since. Space is an unforgiving, violent place, but we're both still here. While Gr'va credits her general distrust of everyone around her as the secret to survival, I can't live like that. Each day my heart still beats is an opportunity to improve my situation, and this research study is the best chance I have to create the life I want. There's no turning back. I need to see this through.

"I'm not stupid," I tell her. "I'll be careful, okay? And if I make it to the end, it'll be worth it."

Gr'va sighs. "Well, I shall pray to the moons that you don't get your innards ripped through your eye sockets by a heavily medicated and twisted creature of Empress Motavvi's creation."

That's as close to a *good luck* as I've ever heard from her. My eyes sting with unshed tears at her genuine well-wishes. "Thank you," I say, trying to swallow my emotions. I open my mouth to tell her I'll miss her, but before I can, she disconnects the call.

It's just as well. I don't like goodbyes anyway.

The rest of the ride is smooth and quiet, allowing me to snooze on and off before landing an hour early on Huva II, which I take as a good omen. Early bird gets the worm and all that.

Huva II's port is abuzz with beings of all species when I deplane, but I keep my eyes on the signs featuring the Cursed Compound's logo—a distorted white castle with an ominous red glow around it—and follow the accompanying arrows through the narrow, hilly cobblestone streets. Eventually, I end up at the back of a very long line that reminds me of the zigzagging lines I'd see at airports back on Earth, though I suppose it also resembles a group of cattle being herded into a slaughterhouse. I blink a few times to refocus my brain on the airport image, since it's less threatening.

The study is open to all species, sizes, genders, and ages, and the line in front of me very much reflects that diversity. I don't recognize the majority of species represented in this queue, but I do notice that I'm the only human here. That's...not ideal.

Due to our short lifespans, humans are often the butt of the joke in space, but if we were too weak to participate in this study, surely they wouldn't allow us to enter. Yet my application was approved, so Empress Motavvi must want more information on the physical, emotional, and mental limitations of the human body.

After a few failed attempts to engage others in line with small talk in Crindan, I decide quiet reflection is the best way to ride out the rest of the wait. I don't take it personally. Well, I *try* not to take it personally. I love chatting with people I don't know, but I'm not everyone's cup of tea. Plus, I seem to be the only one who's happy to be here. The overall vibe from those in line is somber and fearful, and I'm over here giddy as a goat to enter a haunted house I might never leave.

The line moves quickly, and from my view of the entrance, I see that they're letting five people in at a time. Dark-wood double doors creak loudly before each group enters, and I watch closely as they disappear behind the doors and the high, white, concrete-like walls that must be fifty stories tall.

What awaits me behind those walls is sure to frighten the bejesus out of me, and my stomach flips with excitement. I love the thrill of being scared. That rush of adrenaline and not knowing what kind of creature will pop out next is so deliciously fun. And this time, I get paid to wander around dark corners and scream at the top of my lungs. Icing on the cake.

When I finally make it inside, I'm ushered through a series of narrow hallways with sky-blue walls and white marble floors. Then I'm called into a sterile beige room with metal tools lined up neatly atop steel tables and told to strip down to my birthday suit. A trio of three-foot-tall aliens with black scales and silver jumpsuits enters and begins taking samples of my blood and skin as they attach circular discs to the back of my head, under both ears, on my chest, lower back, and on the outside of both knees. They place a pair of light gray pants with an attached woven belt, a matching short-sleeved shirt, and black boots on the only chair in the room, and their erratic hand gestures tell me this will be my uniform for the study.

Not long after I'm dressed, a statuesque creature with orange skin as smooth as glass and Gorgon-like brown hair that looks alive strolls in with a beeping tablet in her hands. She wears the same silver jumpsuit as the others but has the vibe of someone in charge. She looks me up and down—the ends of her hair stretching and wiggling toward the ceiling the whole time—then back to her tablet and nods. "I am Doctor S'Ko. You are now cleared to participate in our study."

Doctor S'Ko leads me out of the room and points to the open auditorium at the end of the hall. "Wait in there. We shall begin shortly."

The doc didn't lie. Within minutes, she steps onto the stage and a hush falls over the crowd. "Welcome all," she says with her three-fingered hands outstretched. "Soon you will enter the Cursed Compound, a revolutionary interactive experience that allows us to monitor your biometrics consistent with your respective species as you go from room to room and encounter creatures from across the universe.

"There are recording devices throughout the compound that will show us what you are doing, and the monitors we placed on your bodies will show us what you are experiencing emotionally and physically while you are inside."

Exhilaration pumps through my blood as she continues to describe the compound. What kinds of monsters will I get to see? Will they be like the standard werewolves, vampires, and creepy crawlies from Earth? Or will they be totally different, like the spindly, goo-covered, three-headed *xorkabeasts* from Gr'va's planet that eat hair?

"Within the compound, there are five different tracks, allowing us to have five of you begin at once. These tracks are similar in design," she explains, "but the empress and I are constantly making improvements and adding new obstacles, so even if you have previously completed a track, you will not be able to predict what lurks behind each door."

She gestures to the screen behind her, and a short list of rules is projected onto it. There are no communication devices or outside weapons allowed, and food and med stations are set up throughout each track to ensure basic needs are met. Once you enter a new room, the door to the previous room locks behind you, so you can't go backward, and you're not even allowed to quit the track. It's finish or die, basically.

The most interesting rule, by far, is the last one, which says we're not allowed to leave the compound with pets or trophies found on the track, and I wonder how many times someone has attempted to smuggle a monster out of this haunted house to take them home.

"There is no time limit to complete your track," Doctor S'Ko says. She clasps her hands in front of her and a slight smile tugs at her lips. "You will encounter other participants on your journey through the compound, and you are allowed to work together, should you choose to do so. There are passageways that allow you to enter another participant's track in the event you would like to form an alliance. This will not disqualify you from earning your credits. The only requirement is to reach the finish line."

We can form alliances? That's a game changer. If I can find someone to partner with, this experience will be a lot easier.

Doctor S'Ko instructs us to follow her out of the auditorium and into the little courtyard area between the high barrier walls and a row of five black doors that look like they lead to a dungeon. Goose bumps race across my skin as I get closer to the front of the line, and the sound of my beating heart rings loudly in my ears, making me fidgety.

When my name is called, I jog the short distance to the starting line, my fists clenching as I wait for my door to open.

This is it. My future lies beyond that door. No matter what I have to face on this track, I'm going to survive so I can claim my credits and finally get the fresh start I've been dreaming of since I was taken.

I can do this. I'm *going* to do this.

CHAPTER 3

KHATAZO

"I can't believe I'm doing this," I say with a wary sigh as I trudge through the iron door and enter the track. It's not my first time participating in a research study for Empress Motavvi, but I hope it's my last.

The previous study I participated in was nine turns around the sun ago, and I was much more agile than I am now. I still have the build of a *P'daki* gladiator, just with the bones of a retired mentor. While my blows remain deadly, my movements have slowed, and my joints ache much sooner than they used to.

I take in the long line of reluctant participants about to enter the Cursed Compound, the scent of fear so thick in the air I almost choke on it. No one wants to be here. I don't blame them. Trauma is born within these eerily clean white walls. If you're lucky enough to make it to the end, you leave with credits, but also nightmares that never fade. This is a quest for funds when no other option avails itself. It's for the desperate, the lonely, the sick, or, for those like me, it's to save the life of someone else.

When I was here last, there were no sustenance or med

stations along the track. If you were injured or hungry, tough. You still had to make it to the end, no matter how much time had passed, or how much blood poured from your open wounds. The monsters I encountered were vicious, and I doubt that has changed with time, but I hope the requirements to unlock the next door are not what they were.

Back then, you needed to kill each beast you faced to advance. The next door didn't unlock until the monster assigned to that room stopped breathing. I still remember the way the small intestines of the *malkuri* I killed stuck to my neck when I draped it over my shoulder. The heat from it against my skin, and worst of all, the way it smelled like rot. We were not given receptacles for these parts to carry them along the track. No, that would be too easy. The empress expected us to carry these severed trophies through the course and deposit them at the end of the track into a large, red bin. The number of parts you finished with determined how many credits you were eligible to receive.

My gladiator training prepared me well for what the empress put us through. I knew how to kill anything in my path quickly and efficiently, but it was never an act I took pleasure in. Those kills, every last one of them, stuck with me. They still do. The fanged *gloper's* heart that continued to beat inside my pocket long after I tore it from his chest cavity. That beat finds me late at night when I'm unable to ease into slumber. And the anguished screams as I tore the *duixa's* head from its body ring in my ears at night, often waking me from sleep to sweat-dampened blankets.

There were over three-hundred participants who entered that study, and I was among the seven who made it out. I finished in record time, and I was the only one who deposited a trophy from each kill. I was praised for it. The empress was impressed by my performance.

I left the compound with enough credits to buy a ship for my crew and keep us fed for an entire turn around the sun, though I could not bring myself to eat anything in the first days that followed.

Alas, the life of a pirate is not a stable one, and jobs in the Crinda Galaxy have waned in recent days. The credits I earn here will pay for the arm amputation Qibor needs after our last job, as well as the cybernetic limb that will be implanted in place of it.

Qibor didn't want me to do this for him. My brother Aukellin also voiced his firm objections once he read the advertisement I found, but we have no other options. I am the strongest among us, we can't take another job with Qibor's injury, and an influx of credits will not come until we take another job. The credits from this study will cover us until my comrade has recovered and we can return to a quieter life of galactic thievery.

This track shouldn't prove difficult. I have heard of the many improvements the empress has made to the compound, and I expect to reach the finish line faster than last time. If she truly has made it easier for participants to complete the track, I plan on shoving my fist through each wall—and face—that stands between me and my credits.

This Doctor S'Ko and her promise of dangerous monsters does not scare me.

The first room I enter is a sustenance station. The overhead lights blind me, and the room is bare except for tables of protein cubes and bags of water. There is a smaller table in the back offering plates of various hallucinogenic drugs in powder form and vials of *wispo*, a sweet, pink liquid found in every debauchery hole in Crinda.

The beverage makes my head fuzzy, and my limbs feel light as air when I drink it. Some species grow stronger and more focused on these substances, but I have no interest in consuming the powder or the *wispo*, as I need my head clear for this endeavor.

I throw back twelve protein cubes and four bags of water, ensuring I'll have enough energy to complete the first few rooms. Hopefully the sustenance stations are plentiful, as I have an appetite to match my large frame. There are tiny sacks the size of my palm dangling on a hook next to the protein cube table, and though only one water bag and a few protein cubes fit inside each, I grab as much as I can, and I stuff the sack before strapping it to my belt and opening the door to the next room.

Sticky air immediately coats my skin and dampens my uniform as I step into the strange, dimly lit conservatory; the humidity so thick, it's hard to breathe. Plants cover the floors, hang from ropes attached to the glass ceiling, and perch on shelves. Their leaves rustle whenever the automatic misting machine turns on, and they let out a quiet, somber squeal when it shuts off.

I have no idea what I'm expected to do in here.

The moment I step toward the door on the far wall and the floor creaks beneath my foot, this room's obstacle becomes clear. The leaves of each plant sway in my direction, and several sets of sharp teeth begin to glow. It's a room full of carnivorous plants, and the only way I can reach the other side is to walk past their open mouths hungry for flesh and try to avoid getting bitten.

"*Fiyk,*" I groan, then take a deep inhale and charge toward the exit. Multiple sets of fangs sink into my forearms, stomach, and legs, cutting through my uniform, and I grit my teeth to keep from howling in pain. I raise my arms above my head to cover my face, and flesh is torn from my body with each step.

The plants grow more desperate to make me their meal, and

I have to slap away the wide, bright yellow leaves that hang in my face, blocking my view of the door. The sting from the plants' venom is crippling as it settles into my blood, and I can hear the quiet sizzle of my flesh burning away as an agonized groan escapes me. My knees start to buckle, the pain so intense.

I can't allow the first room of Empress Motavvi's compound to best me. It would be humiliating. Aukellin would be merciless in his mockery.

Steeling my spine, I clench my fists and sink my fangs into the inside of my cheek, creating a new source of pain to distract from the burning wounds covering my body. Reaching for the closest plant, my hand wraps around several stems and I pull. A wailing cry follows the moment its roots separate from the soil, and I can't help but smile at the plant's demise.

I tear myself from the plants currently latched onto my calf and duck just as a plant with spiky, rectangular leaves speckled with bright red spots drops its head and attempts to bite my nose. With the back of my hand, I slap it away, and it flies off its shelf.

A tall plant hanging from the ceiling hisses down at me, its blue petals darkening with what must be rage. I have killed some of its friends, and now it seems ready to avenge them. But I don't relent. I hiss back as I continue to pound the leaves that rustle in front of me, rip the roots from their cozy, dampened quarters, and the pots that contain their life forces flip, their contents spilling over the floor like the blood of past foes.

As I reach for the handle of the door, potted teal flowers aim their petals upward, and hot liquid shoots from the center of their ovules, hitting me in the eye. I let out a loud bellow as I claw at my eyes, desperately trying to wipe them clean. My vision is blurred as I feel along the wall for the door. Panicked that I have permanently lost my sight, I drop my right shoulder and slam my body into the obstacle. The wood splinters, and I fall forward onto the thin carpet of the next room.

Rolling onto my back, I squint just as a cooling spray shoots down from the ceiling and covers my face. It cleans enough of the burning substance from my eyes that colors and shapes return before me, and I can just make out the broken slabs of the door folding back into place until it is solid once more.

Despite the lingering pain and cloudy vision, I spring to my feet, preparing for the next threat, only to find large, colorful blocks scattered across the white carpet. In the middle of the blocks is a deep, diamond-shaped box carved into the floor.

"A puzzle," I growl.

I *despise* puzzles. An extraordinary waste of time, they are. Does Empress Motavvi wish to study my ability to snap the bones of other creatures like kindling or fiddle with strange shapes, trying to make them fit together? If mental endurance is something she wishes to research, then there should be a separate track with mind exercises such as this.

I'm capable of completing puzzles in a short amount of time. It's just that I choose not to. The most impressive part of me is not my mind, it's my body. My brute strength. It's why I was such a celebrated gladiator, why I was one of only seven to complete the track the last time. My brother Aukellin was also a gladiator, but he enjoys activities requiring patience and deep thinking. Perhaps he should have volunteered for this study instead of me.

A tapping sound pulls my attention to the left, and I discover a small female on the other side of a glass wall dividing my track from hers. I've never seen another like her. She bangs on the glass with her tiny fist, trying to get my attention, and when our eyes meet, she smiles. She is strange to behold. Her face is flat and smooth, with a large forehead and a nose so narrow it looks as if it would fold in on itself with a flick of my finger.

No protective plating covers her ample chest and round stomach, and I see no fins protruding from wrists or ankles to help her navigate rough waters. Perhaps she has retractable parts that keep her safe, because if not, I don't know how this female has survived this long.

Her voice is muffled by the thickness of the glass, but she shouts, "Hey! Me and you, work together?" in Crindan. She points to her chest. "I'm Ehrn," which, I assume, is her name.

I wave my hand away, dismissing her offer for teamwork. Doctor S'Ko said working with other participants in this study is allowed, but that doesn't mean I have interest in such pursuits. Besides, of the many beings I could partner with, this weak, ugly female is the last I would choose.

Ehrn rolls her eyes in frustration and returns to the obstacle on her track. She seems to be in a puzzle room like I am, but hers has much smaller pieces, all black, and her hands work quickly as she gathers the pieces and sticks them into the frame on the wall.

For a moment, I watch her to determine whether her puzzle is like mine, but her frame is an entirely different shape, as are the pieces she picks up with her many fingers.

Letting out a growl, I smash my foot into the frame of the puzzle, hoping I may trick it into rendering the puzzle complete. When that doesn't work, I return my focus to assembling it the preferred way. I must complete this if I wish to move farther on the track. Hauling the large purple piece into my arms, I drop it onto the floor in the center of the frame and shift it horizontally until the puzzle frame lights up and lets out a pleasant-sounding beep to indicate it's in the right spot. It takes longer to get the green piece to fit, and sweat runs down the sides of my face by the time I lift the red piece off the floor.

Banging on the glass has me looking up to see Ehrn smiling widely at me once again, displaying her many square, blunt teeth. The door to the next room is ajar, and I wonder why she has not moved on. "I'm good at puzzles!" she shouts. Ehrn gestures between her chest and mine. "Let's be allies."

I shake my head, again declining. Mind-bending puzzles are not where my strengths lie, but still, I wish to complete this track alone.

She shrugs and strides confidently through the open door, and I'm left wondering, for the briefest of moments, if I shall regret not making her my ally.

"No," I say quietly. No, I'm stronger on my own. I am *P'daki*, a former gladiator, and a pirate. The most ferocious monster in this compound. Whatever lies ahead should fear *me*.

CHAPTER 4

ERIN

When I exit the puzzle room, I find myself in a darkened closet with only a ladder that leads to the floor above. I reach around, looking for a light switch, but I find nothing. The ladder is silver and gleams slightly in the dark, so I can climb without clear sight, but I can't tell where the latch is on the trap door that'll get me out of here.

Oh well. It's not like I'm on a time limit.

I try to picture that rude red guy in here and have to stifle a laugh. He probably wouldn't even fit in this room unless he entered sideways or something.

No one enjoys the feeling of rejection, and while my ego is certainly bruised, it's probably for the best. Having an ally of his size, covered in bulging muscles, sure would've been handy, especially if I need to defeat a monster on a high shelf, but who knows if he has any useful skills beyond the brawn. Putting that puzzle together, he looked like a pig on ice.

Holding onto the bar mere centimeters from my face, I begin to climb. About halfway up, I look to the ceiling and find myself the same distance from the top as I was before I started climbing. How is that possible? Is it an optical illusion? Or is this the trick of the room? I remember a machine at the gym like this, and I avoided it like the plague. Who wants to climb a ladder to nowhere?

This is some top-notch torment. Pointless cardio in a room the size of a sardine can is an absolute nightmare. My thighs burn as I continue my ascent, and a soft creak is the only warning I get before a pair of thick forearms covered in open wounds bursts through the wall behind me, and a hand with cracked, dark brown fingernails wraps around my ankle.

I let out a surprised shriek and start kicking the hand with my free foot as I clutch the rung of the ladder. "No, no, no!" I shout as my grip loosens and I dangle from the ladder with one hand. Slamming the heel of my boot into the back of the hand, I hear a pained grunt before the grip loosens and the arms disappear back behind the wall. I quickly right myself on the ladder and hustle up the rungs like a squirrel being chased by a dog.

I make it up several more rungs and notice that I'm finally closer to the trap door on the ceiling, when another set of arms blasts through the wall in front of me. The ladder is the only thing that separates my neck from the fingers seeking it. Leaning back as far as I can, I swing my shoulders side to side, avoiding their grasp. From this angle, I'm able to get a better look at those arms, and...ick. The skin is gray and mottled with bruises. There are jagged scars circling both wrists, and the blood that seeps from the open gashes appears to be black.

Something moves beneath the skin, and I bite my lip to keep from screaming. It's a horrifying sight, made a million times worse when movement makes its way to the edge of the wound and the wiggling body of a worm inches its way out.

Bile rises in my throat, and I feel like I've reached my limit, horror-wise. I didn't see anything in that advertisement about animated zombie arms stuffed with bugs. Nope. No, thank you.

I need to get out of here before I drown that worm in vomit and those disgusting hands choke the life out of me.

Shifting my focus back to the task at hand, I resume my climb. I get into a rhythm, my feet and hands moving quicker than I thought possible. I narrowly escape another zombie-arm attack from the wall to my left and start pounding on the trap door the second I reach it.

When that doesn't work, I slide my palm across the wood, looking for a latch. Eventually, I find it, and huff with exertion as I push it open and pull myself through, flopping onto my side as I try to catch my breath. It takes a beat for me to notice my surroundings, but when I do, I rub my eyes to make sure I'm not hallucinating.

"A slide? Really?" I mutter to no one. A bright yellow, curly slide fills the room, surrounded by the low-hanging branches of trees that remind me of the huge, live oaks that grew in Granny's backyard. This room looks more like a playground than something you'd find in a haunted house, but I'm not complaining. It's better than zombie arms, that's for damn sure.

I scoot my booty toward the mouth of the slide, peering down to determine the catch, because there's gotta be a catch, right? Empress Motavvi and Doctor S'Ko don't seem generous enough to provide a break in the action like this. Taking a deep breath, I tuck my arms in and press my fists beneath my chin before pushing off the edge. My stomach flips as I whip around the first curve, and the sweet innocence of childhood comes rushing back. But I'm no fool. I keep my eyes open as I scan the room. This becomes a struggle when the first low branch blocks my periphery, and I have to duck to avoid it smacking me in the face.

The further down I go, the more branches hang low over the slide, and they become impossible to avoid. It's not the branches that pose the real threat though. It's the webs that stretch between the leaves.

"Ugh!" I cry out. Frantically, I claw at my hair and face as I fly through the first web. The silken threads feel like they're everywhere—on the tip of my nose, across my eyelids, even in my mouth, and as quickly as I scrape one off, I glide beneath another branch and my head and face are covered.

Then I want to kick myself for not realizing sooner that I should just lay flat to remain web-free. Once I do that, the views from the slide become much prettier. I don't spot any spiders, but with the number of webs in here, you'd think they'd be everywhere.

I don't notice I'm nearing the end of the slide until my feet smack into a bendy clear divider, kind of like a big doggie door, and I'm deposited with a loud thump onto a nubby blue carpet in a narrow hallway. What lies in front of me is a white door labeled "Sustenance Station."

I'm not expecting a four-course meal on the other side of that door, but something to remove the remaining bits of web from my hair would be a damn miracle.

Once my hair is clean, I take my time, slowly eating the dry, flavorless protein cubes as my thoughts drift to the giant red alien who blew me off. Everything about him was very alien, but he was also kind of cute. The way his long, seafoam-green hair hung in silky strands around his broad shoulders, the shimmer of his red scales whenever the light hit them, and the width of his nose paired with the gold barbell piercing at the bridge of it made him look like he's in a permanent state of crabbiness. There was also a bump in the middle of his nose that gave him a rugged look. Like he's been in more than a few bar fights.

I'd guess he's at least seven and a half feet tall, and the bones on his shoulders and elbows stick out in sharp and intimidating ways, but I sensed a gentleness in him, a vulnerable side that he tries to keep hidden. Maybe that's just wishful thinking on my part—I'm a sucker for a scarred cinnamon roll—but the way he scratched his head as he stared at the puzzle pieces and tilted his head side to side as he formulated a plan reminded me of a dog hearing the word "treat" or "park."

I gulp a bag of water as I wander toward the back of the room where there are plates of drugs and little bottles of booze. My stomach can't handle *wispo*, and I've gotten sick from it enough times to know to abstain, but I take three nips and stuff them into one of the canvas totes they have hanging up and tie the handles through my belt loop. Maybe I can use my own projectile vomit as a weapon of some kind. You never know.

The next room I enter has a floor made of sand and two ropes strung from this side of the room stretching to the far side, one up high, and one about a foot above the ground. It looks like the space version of a volleyball court, but since there's no ball to be found, and because I wasn't born in a barn, I know there's gotta be more to it than that.

There has to be something terrifying under the top layer of sand, and I have no interest in getting bitten by alien crabs, so rather than walk across the sand to reach the door, I step onto the bottom rope and grab the rope above my head to steady me. Two steps across the rope are all I get before my foot slips, and I fall onto the sand. I *really* should've put more effort into perfecting the pull-up. Even being able to do one would come in handy right now.

Keeping one hand on the bottom rope, I pinch my eyes closed and wait for bugs to start crawling all over me, but they don't come. Instead, I notice the muddy, clay-like bottom of the sandpit and the way it's rapidly sucking me into its depths.

"Quicksand? Why?" I shout toward the sky. My hand never leaves the rope, and my other hand flails as panic sets in.

What do I do? How do I get out of this?

I wish I could remember the cartoons of my youth that made quicksand seem like a national crisis, popping up in every town, swallowing curious children whole.

The only thing I can remember is that you're not supposed to panic like I'm doing right now. But how am I supposed to stay calm when the clay feels like it's hardening around my feet as it pulls me in?

Going against every instinct, I stop kicking my feet and twist my body just enough so I can get both hands on the rope. Facing the side of the room allows me to look through the glass wall at my big, red friend.

I'm surprised to find him watching me. His yellow eyes with vertical slits don't blink as they remain locked on me, and he has one hand pressed against the glass, the webbing between his fingers so fascinating that it temporarily distracts me from the fact that I'm slowly drowning in dirt.

Tightening my grip on the rope, I pinch my eyes closed and take a few deep breaths. I don't have much upper body strength, but I summon all that I can to pull myself out. That gets me barely an inch out of the sand, and I have to bite my lip to keep from crying hopelessly.

I don't want him to see me like this. Only a couple rooms into the compound, weepy and about to be buried alive.

Slow and steady, I tell myself. *One inch at a time.*

As I'm trying to haul my butt out, I end up moving along the length of the rope, and if I'm caked in mud from the waist down for the rest of the track, I'm fine with that. Just as long as I get the heck outta this room.

I'm grunting and sweaty and maybe only three inches out of the sand by the time I'm halfway down the rope, and my gaze drifts back to Big Red. I could swear he looks slightly impressed.

He probably thought I'd be dead by now with my weak human arms and tissue-paper skin.

I'll show him.

About a foot from the end of the rope, I manage to get one leg free, and it's just close enough that I can lift myself out and get my foot planted beyond the edge of the quicksand pit. It gives me enough leverage to climb all the way out. I flop onto my back, and laughter escapes my lips at the realization that I defeated quicksand, and I know seven-year-old me would be very proud.

I look over at Big Red, hoping he's on his knees, ready to eat crow for underestimating me, but the room he was in is completely empty.

A bone-chilling roar fills the air, shaking the glass wall separating my track from his, and I launch myself toward the door. I don't need his name to know that scream was his, and I can't let him face whatever it is alone.

CHAPTER 5

KHATAZO

I must applaud the efforts of Empress Motavvi and Doctor S'Ko. The last study I participated in was a challenge in strength and brutality, but this...this is a test of true psychological torment. The room I'm in looks like nothing more than an empty hallway with peeling wallpaper, a handful of portraits on each side, and a dingy carpet that appears to have old blood splatters covering it.

Of course I suspected it wouldn't be as easy as walking from one end of the hallway to the other, but I didn't expect to be on my knees, sobbing into my palms this soon.

I have encountered spirits before, but they were not this horrifying. I have no idea how the empress did it, but she made it so the spirits that emerge from the portraits on the wall look and sound like the loved ones I've lost.

My father seeped out of the frame of his portrait, called my name, and admonished me for becoming a professional thief. My younger brother, Vixato, who was mauled to death by a *rom tuk qi* beast in the arena, appears from the second frame and begs for death.

Over and over, he pleads with me to pierce his heart, and I

know he speaks not to me. These are the last words he ever spoke. His fight versus the *rom tuk qi* beast was highly anticipated and broadcast across the planet. Those in the arena heard him beg for death and cheered with exuberance when the beast wasted no time in granting his wish.

But here in this haunted hallway, his words repeat. His voice cracks on the blood bubbling in his throat, and he lets out a choked sob as he waits for his own heart to stop beating. I can't imagine anything more gut-wrenching could come out of these portraits, but there are many left between my body and the door, and I fall to my knees, clutching the sides of my skull as Vixato moans, "Please. Please, no more."

I crawl a bit farther along the carpet, and Vixato's voice begins to fade. It feels like a victory, enough so that I'm able to breathe again. A heartbeat later, my mother's voice reaches my ears, and it shatters my remaining resolve.

She cries out for me, telling me to care for my brothers as she knows she will no longer be able to. These are the words she spoke before she was decapitated in the town square in front of me, Vixato, and Aukellin by the king who led his army into our atmosphere, landed on our shores, and slaughtered our people.

"Tazo, keep them safe!" my mother's spirit shouts.

An anguished roar rips free of my lungs and fills the air. I press my palms into my eyes, refusing to look at the horror on her face, but I see it clearly in my memories anyway.

The Bugoros took our planet and made my people their slaves. Me, my brothers, and a handful of other strong males were spared a life of servitude only because the king thought we would be better as entertainers inside the arena. When not fighting for our lives, we were forced to live in cramped underground cages beneath it. When we were victorious, our bodies were offered to the wives of politicians and guardsmen the king worked closely with. My body was no longer my own. It was a tool, or a prop, to be used however the king wished.

My mother's spirit does not relent as she continues her tearful plea. "Do not let them watch."

I did as she asked that day, covering Vixato's eyes, while Aukellin kept his gaze on the stone beneath his feet as tears streamed down his cheeks.

If this is what I am to expect of the rest of this track, I don't think I can go on. Though the empress will not allow me to quit. How will I endure this level of torture if there's more ahead? I would sooner impale myself on a sword than be forced to listen to my loved ones utter their final words.

Black spots appear at the corners of my vision, and the room sways around me. It feels as if the walls begin to move, inching closer to me on either side. I shouldn't be surprised. The only thing worse than listening to my family cry out in pain is to be forced into a tight, confined space, and, of course, the empress has figured out a way to weaponize my greatest fear.

"N-no. No more," I mumble, my speech slurring as I press my forehead into the dirty carpet.

"Get up!" a voice shouts.

Relief washes over me when it's a voice I don't recognize.

"Come on, Big Red," the voice says again. "It's not like I can carry that two-ton tush of yours. Get. Up."

Wait, I do recognize this voice. It is the ugly female from the other side of the glass. Ehrn, I think she is called. When I lift my head to look at her, the light from the ceiling casts a glow around her head like a halo.

She has come to save me?

There's an empty frame toward the end of the hall that is hanging ajar, as if it's a secret door. That must be how Ehrn reached me from her track.

Her green eyes roll at my reluctance to follow her orders,

and she stomps toward the middle of the hall. There, she places a vial of *wispo* on the carpet, opens her arms wide over her head, and utters a string of words I do not recognize.

The translucent faces of my family swirl around her, along with several others I've never seen before, continuing to howl their tales of woe, but she appears unfazed. She drops a second vial next to the first and repeats the words again.

"What are you doing?" I ask.

A moment later, the spirits evaporate and silence fills the hallway. She rushes back to my side and tugs my hand. "We need to move. Now!"

In a daze, I stumble to my feet and let her pull me toward the door. Once we're on the other side, we slam the door closed and lean our backs against it, side by side and breathless.

Ehrn turns to me and says, "Since I just saved your butt, wanna be partners?"

Reluctantly, I nod. It's not as if I have any reason or leverage to refuse her help. She is better at this than I. The thought embarrasses me, but I can deny the truth of it no longer.

"What did you do in there?" I ask.

"Hmm?"

"To rid the spirits?"

She waves her hand dismissively. "Oh, my sister was a witch. She made potions and cast spells since we were little. She said our granny's house had bad energy upstairs, so on every full moon, she'd steal a bottle of liquor from the kitchen, recite a spell, and leave it at the top of the steps as an offering." Ehrn sighs wistfully. "She swore it worked, so I figured I'd give it a try. I can't believe I still remember the words."

"What did you see upon entering the room?" I ask, unable to refrain. "Were there spirits from your past?"

She nods but does not elaborate. Creases form on her flat brow, and the look in her eyes is tormented. Could her past somehow be more traumatic than my own? How did she manage to maintain the composure required to save me?

Ehrn shrugs. "Everyone has ghosts."

I don't know what to say to that.

"Huh," Ehrn says, taking in the room we're in now. She pushes off the door. "I was just in a sustenance station, but I guess I should be thankful for all the breaks we get, right?"

I clear my throat and follow her to a table with med supplies. "Yes, this is a welcome respite."

She stands on tiptoes and grabs my chin, turning my face side to side. The scent of her mane fills my nose, and it reminds me of freshly fallen rain over the flower fields during the hot season. "Looks like you could use some bandages."

I grunt in agreement as I look down at the scratches covering my arms, the fabric of my shirt now in tatters from the carnivorous plants.

"What's your name?" she asks with an amused chuckle. "Or do you prefer I keep calling you Big Red?"

"I'm called Khatazo," I reply. "You are Ehrn?"

"Yeah, that's me."

She smiles as her gaze meets mine, and this time, I find her blunt teeth somewhat endearing. I wonder how she is able to eat and if her body is getting the nutrition it needs. Perhaps she liquefies her food. It's a shame she recently ate because it would be fascinating to witness her trying to chew on a protein cube.

And her eyes. They are bottomless pools of green that remind me of the ponds near the home where I grew up.

Other beings mill about the room, paying us no mind and chatting as they wander from the protein cube table to the water bags. A few even lean over the drug plates and inhale neat lines of the powder through their nostrils.

It's strange to see so many others in here, as my track has been empty other than the ability to see Ehrn through the wall.

Then I notice four doors along the walls in addition to the one she and I came through, and I realize this must be a communal sustenance station that all tracks lead to.

"Now that we're allies, care to share what made you sign up for this study?" Ehrn asks as she rubs sticky blue ointment over my open wounds.

Normally, I wouldn't be inclined to share personal information, but since we're allies, I suppose there's no harm in telling her. "My crewmate. Qibor. The credits from this study will get him the medical attention he needs."

"That's nice of you," she says, impressed. "Your *crew*? Are you in the military?"

I laugh at her words. "No, my pursuits aren't that noble. I'm a pirate."

The thick lines of tiny fur above her eyes lift, and I am mystified by the way her pupils expand.

"You're a pirate?" she asks excitedly. "That's cool."

"That's not the word I would use to describe my profession," I tell her. "It's often dangerous and unpredictable."

"So you just fly around the galaxy stealing buckets of rare jewels?"

I shake my head. "We have not encountered any *buckets of jewels* lately, which is why I'm here. Though, if you have wealthy friends, I would appreciate their exact coordinates."

She chuckles, the sound reminding me of bells—light and cheerful. I suddenly feel the desperate urge to touch her skin. I wonder if it's as smooth as it looks.

I lift my knuckles, brushing them along her cheek, and I hear her breath hitch at the contact. It's as smooth as sea glass, and as I run the pad of my thumb across the line of her jaw, my cock hardens at the thought of touching her elsewhere.

Ehrn isn't ugly like I previously thought. She is different. Her skin is the color of milk, but when she's nervous—like she is now—her cheeks and neck pinken like a *Ratchutahzi* sunset. Though her stature is small compared to mine, she is round and soft all over, making me want to sink my hands into her abundant flesh, kneading and gripping her most sensitive parts until she is writhing with need.

"Apologies," I say, letting my hand drop to my side. "Your skin does not seem adequate. It's far too delicate to protect your vital organs."

"Preaching to the choir, buddy," she says with a weary sigh. "I'd give anything for some protective plating around my noggin."

Her words make no sense, but her expressions are so animated when she speaks, I can look nowhere else.

"And I still get bacne. Can you believe that? At thirty-six. That nonsense should be behind me."

"What is back-nee?"

She scoffs. "If you don't know what it is, you've clearly never had to deal with it, and for that, be thankful."

Ehrn bends at the waist and applies the ointment to a long gash across my calf. From this angle, I notice the outline of her thick, luscious bottom, and I run my tongue along the sharp points of my fangs as I envision biting into it.

"Why are you in this study?" I ask, subtly adjusting my pants to keep my throbbing cock from poking her in the face.

Thankfully she does not look up as she answers. "I'm tired of the life I've got, so I figured I'd come here, score some credits, and buy myself a fresh start."

I understand this desire. "This fresh start of yours, the credits you earn will be enough?"

She covers the gash on my calf with one of the rubbery bandages and shrugs. "I think so. I don't need much, just a roof over my head in a place that's quiet and safe."

A laugh escapes me. I can't help it. "You plan to find this

roof of safety in Crinda? With no mate to protect you?" I ask. Her goal is lofty and unrealistic.

Ehrn's gaze turns cold as she finishes applying the ointment to a cut across my knee, then rises to her feet. "Why is that funny?" She folds her arms across her chest, pressing her teats together in a way that makes my mouth water. "I'll have you know, Yeronix just reopened its borders and is currently allowing humans to settle there, including unmated humans. The ad specifically said unmated humans were welcome. The credits I get from this will be more than enough to buy a house and cover my expenses as I get settled."

"Yeronix?" I ask, unable to keep my jaw from falling open. She could not have chosen a worse planet. "Empress Motavvi rules Yeronix. The same empress who created this insidious compound. You think she'll welcome you without conditions?"

Her lips part, and I expect a cutting retort, but she says nothing.

Guilt fills my chest as I watch the bravado leave her body. I have hurt her, but I'd rather her heart be hurt by my words than her delicate human bones be broken by whatever nefarious creatures the empress lets roam freely on Yeronix.

"It's a trap, Ehrn," I say, softening my tone. "Yeronix has long been a beacon for pitiful souls such as yours, desperately seeking freedom. A safe place, that does not make it. I've seen it with my own eyes. It's a lawless trash heap."

Ehrn's fire returns, and she jabs me in the chest with two of her little fingers. "Did you just call me pitiful?"

Did I? *"Fiyk,"* I mutter the moment I realize I did use that word. "That's not what—"

My words are cut off by the sudden presence of red fog entering the room through narrow cracks along the floor. It billows around us like a cloud made of blood, and my head turns dizzy as I breathe it in.

Ehrn coughs as she waves a frantic hand in front of her face, trying to clear it away.

The fog fills the room. So much so, I no longer see the other beings strolling about. I see nothing beyond the fog. Instinctively, I grab hold of Ehrn's shoulders and pull her into my arms. A relieved sigh whooshes out of me at my ability to still see her flat face.

She places a hand on the part of my chest where my shirt is torn, and her touch sets my skin ablaze. A hunger builds at the base of my spine, a hunger that only the press of Ehrn's body can satisfy. I want to taste her skin. I want to run my tongue along her neck to see if she is as sweet as she smells.

"Khatazo? I...um," she whispers, her heavy-lidded gaze dropping to my lips. She sinks her flat teeth into her plush bottom lip, and my cock hardens against my thigh, making my pants uncomfortably tight.

Before I can lean down and press my mouth to hers, the fog clears, and the others in the room become visible once more. Two males mate rigorously in one corner, and in another is a female surrounded by males. She has a cock in her mouth, one in her cunt, and the other male's mouth leaves a wet trail across her teats. Two females near us claw at each other's skin while a male looks on with his cock in hand, and three other males snarl as they continue to inhale the drug powder.

The fog is causing this mating frenzy. There's no other explanation. Mere moments ago, every being in this room was focused on finishing the track and collecting the credits from this study. Now, they are drunk on desire and giving in to those urges.

It must be why Ehrn continues to touch and look at me as if I'm the only male in the universe capable of giving her pleasure. It also explains why my cock is throbbing to the point of pain, my sac tight against my body, ready to burst.

For the barest fraction of a second, I consider feeding this need I have for her and pressing her against the wall as I drive into her wet heat. I envision the explicit bliss of her walls squeezing around me as she screams my name, her cunt milking me as I fill her soft, supple body with my seed.

But when the males by the drug table drop their empty plates to the floor and step toward us, I shove Ehrn behind me and rip off the tattered remains of my shirt, freeing my arms of any constrictions before letting out a sharp warning hiss.

I am bigger than all three of these males. I'm not concerned about winning this battle. It is Ehrn and her weak human body that worry me. If one of these males gets close enough to swipe their claws along her skin, she will bleed out. That cannot happen. I need her. There is no chance I'll be able to finish this track without her.

I also suspect Ehrn needs me too. We are a team, and I shall do what is necessary to keep her safe from harm.

"What are you doing?" Ehrn shouts from behind me.

I have no time to explain, so I yell, "Stay down. I won't let them touch you."

It's clear to me now that she's the mentally stronger competitor of the two of us, and if the only way I can contribute to this alliance is through violence, then I shall slaughter every creature that stands in our path.

The males close in on us, and my fangs lengthen inside my mouth until I taste blood. They launch themselves at me, all three at once, and I welcome them with sharpened claws.

CHAPTER 6
ERIN

I can't see what's happening. In fact, I can't see much of anything beyond the broad expanse of Khatazo's back, but if the hisses, growls, and loud, wet thuds are any indication of what's going on, I'm thankful for my big, red blind spot.

A furry gray limb flies toward the corner of the room, blood spurting out of it like a squirt gun, and a pained howl immediately follows. I didn't even notice the creatures that Khatazo is currently tearing apart before they attacked, but that's probably because I was in a horned-up daze and only had eyes for my ally.

It's been a long time since I've been attracted to anyone. I had a small crush on a server at The Meat Pocket, but it went away the day he told me he had five mates who all had eggs in their bellies that were about to hatch. I don't even like eating eggs, so the thought of growing one and it hatching inside me, scratching up my organs when it cracked, freaked me the heck out.

Gr'va bought me a vibrator last year, but she got it at the

station's pawnshop, and it had so many buttons and sharp edges that I was afraid to put it anywhere near my lady parts. I used it as a white noise machine instead.

But Khatazo, mmm-mmm-mmm. He's a tall drink of lemonade. This might be the red fog talking—no, it's *definitely* the red fog talking—but I kind of want to run my tongue all over his body and ride his face until I pass out.

A howl roars from him as he rips the head off a boar-like creature with burnt-yellow tusks. The boar-man's body folds in on itself in an awkward heap at Khatazo's feet, and he kicks it away, sending the corpse across the room. It lands on the table of water bags, popping most of them. The table collapses beneath the weight, and a watery red puddle forms on the floor.

I become entranced by the flex of his back muscles as the fight continues, and I can't stop myself from reaching my hand out to touch his skin. He tenses at my touch and stops punching long enough to ask, "Ehrn, are you hurt?"

He says my name like "urn," and I'm surprised by how hot I find it. Who knew the name of a vase filled with dead-people dust could sound so sexy? The concern in his voice sends a kaleidoscope of somersaulting butterflies through my belly, which conjures an odd image, but the butterflies are definitely not casually flying around. These butterflies are high on red fog, and their wings are flapping crazy fast. Much like the beat of my heart.

Eventually the growling and wet thuds cease, and Khatazo turns to face me. He's covered in blood, sweat, and lots of other things I'm not sure I want identified, and I've never wanted anyone more. His eyes search my face as he grabs my shoulders, then he looks me up and down. "Are you well?"

"Yes," I moan. I'm breathless, and I don't know what to do about it. This desire is so intense that my clit is throbbing, but as much as I want Khatazo to strip me bare and take me right here and now, I can't let that happen. If I do, I'll never know if I really want him or if it's just the fog.

Not that I expect to stay in touch with him once we leave the compound. He's a pirate, and I want a quiet life in the middle of nowhere—Yeronix, preferably. I don't care what he says about the empress. Unless I get some proof that Yeronix isn't safe, I'm still going there once this is over. This partnership with Khatazo and I won't extend past the borders of Huva II, and I need to remember that.

"Here," I tell him, taking his hand in mine and leading him to the side of the water table not damaged by a monster corpse. "Let's get you cleaned up." There are four unpopped bags, and I use those to rinse the blood from Khatazo's hands and chest.

"Thanks," I eventually say as he tosses three protein cubes into his mouth at once. "For saving me."

He stares at me, then gestures between the two of us. "Allies," is all he says, and part of me wonders if that's all we are and if I'm okay with that.

There are still a few couples having sex in the room as we leave, and I'm amazed that the pile of dead bodies and severed limbs did nothing to kill their lust. It's impressive really.

The next room we enter isn't a room at all. It's a hallway with a wide, wooden staircase that ascends several floors. Poking my head over the banister, I try counting the floors above us, but I lose track after twelve. "What is the point of this? To get us in shape?"

"You think there is nothing to do here but climb?" Khatazo asks with a chuckle as he runs a hand through his silky hair.

He makes a good point. There's gotta be more to this than meets the eye. With a sigh, I begin the climb. "Onward and upward."

My breath comes out in ragged huffs by the time we reach the first landing, and I lean heavily on the banister, but the moment my skin meets the surface of the wood, I yank my hand back with a gasp. "Ugh," I groan as I take in the wet, brownish-black liquid covering my palm. "Is that...blood?"

Khatazo leans in and sniffs my hand. He grunts, puzzled, before his forked tongue pops out and he gives it a taste. Nodding, he says, "Yes, it is." He tilts his head to the side and adds, "Fresh, it seems."

Disgusted, I bend down and frantically wipe the blood on the leg of my pants. "Why would you do that?"

He scowls at me. "How else would I be able to determine what it is?"

I shake my head, knowing that his question doesn't require a verbal response. I'll just chalk it up to extreme cultural differences. At least the panic over the bloody banister distracted me from my exhaustion.

We step toward the door at the top of the landing, but before Khatazo reaches for the knob, it whips open and a man with snow-white skin, dark circles beneath his eyes, shaggy and tangled brown hair, and sharp fangs dripping with blood leaps out at us. I don't realize I'm shrieking until the vampire puts a hand over one ear and winces. The look on his face is so surprisingly adorable that my shriek turns into a belly-deep laugh.

"Good scare, my man," I say in Crindan. "You really got me there." I pat him on the shoulder. "Fantastic job."

"Ehrn, do not touch him!" Khatazo shouts, pulling me behind him.

"Is that makeup?" I ask the vampire, peeking around Khatazo's bulky arm as my gaze drifts over his twisted features, the deep scars down his neck that disappear behind the high, ruffled collar of his shirt, and the blood that's smeared around his mouth. "Or is that your real face?"

He blinks at me while letting out a menacing groan, and I wonder if he's offended, or if he just doesn't speak Crindan.

"I'm sorry," I begin. "I didn't mean there was something wrong with your face. I just meant...See, my mom used to work at a haunted house, and my sister and I would hang around during her shifts, and—"

My explanation is interrupted by the loud cracking sound of Khatazo's foot blasting through the banister. Wood splinters around us. I don't notice the sharp stake in his hand until he plunges it through the vampire's heart. There's a flash of horror in the vampire's black eyes as he realizes the end is nigh, then his body explodes like a water balloon being stuck with a pin. But instead of water shooting out, it's blood.

I stand there, holding up my hands, not breathing, as I look down at the brownish-black liquid dripping from my fingers.

"Ah," Khatazo says with a nod, "that is where the blood came from."

Frustration mounts as I look from Khatazo's blood-covered hands back to my own, and I can't help but think this blood shower could've been avoided if Khatazo had even an ounce of patience in his giant body. "Why did you do that? We were in the middle of a conversation."

"No," he says, "*you* were in the middle of rambling meaningless details about your past to a creature intent on killing us."

"He could've been an actor!" I shout. "At the haunted houses on Earth, they were all actors wearing costumes and makeup. You don't know why he was here. He could've been one of the participants. Or maybe he was forced to work here and didn't actually want to hurt anyone."

Khatazo sighs heavily as he wipes the back of his hand across his forehead and flings spots of blood across the wall. "Ehrn, we do not have time to learn why each monster we encounter is here, and the reason doesn't matter. We must destroy them and move on."

Memories flood my mind of the days when Mom worked at the local haunted house, and how it was the only job she could hold onto because it was seasonal, didn't require any level of focus, and she could be high on the job without anyone noticing since she was dressed like a zombie and the only thing expected of her was to lurch around making weird noises. It worked for her, and the money she made from it ensured that our bellies were full, even if just for a few months out of the year.

She wasn't an actor like many of her coworkers were, but they embraced her with open arms, even knowing about her addiction. They embraced us too and took turns watching us during their lunch breaks. They would sneak us food from the snack booth, they'd let us play dress up in their costumes, and they never yelled at us when we got into their makeup and made a huge mess. Even Miss Mae the Mummy—who worked there the longest and whose last name we never learned— would bring us homemade lasagna and old clothes her granddaughter had grown out of.

In fact, I had plans to fly back to Philly to celebrate Miss Mae's ninety-third birthday, but the night before my trip, I was kidnapped.

Honestly, I never felt safer than when I was at that haunted house surrounded by monsters.

I know this is different, but does my ally have to be such a colossal turd about it?

"Sorry I took thirty seconds out of my life to pay that vampire a compliment," I mutter coldly as I stride toward the next set of stairs. "I'll be more like you from now on. You know, just slashing throats and constantly growling like the entire universe is out to get me."

"We are inside the Cursed Compound," he says with a chuckle, as if my visible rage is amusing somehow, which makes me even angrier. "Every being that we face *is* out to get us. That's the point of this study."

"Actually, the point of this study is to gauge our reactions when faced with a threat," I correct him, smug as heck that I finally get the chance to be right. "They want to see what we do in order to get from one room to the next. Killing everyone we come across isn't required. You assume it's necessary to make it out of here, but it might not be. Did you ever think of that?"

His mouth falls open, and I can't tell if he's blown away by my insight, or if he's milliseconds away from taking a bite out of me.

"Of course not," I continue, enjoying this high too much to stop chasing it. "Because everyone is evil and you're the only smart one and nothing is worth your time if it doesn't suit your needs."

His features twist into a deep scowl, and I could swear his cheeks turn a darker shade of red than the rest of him.

"Ah, and here comes the temper. That Khatazo dazzle. You gonna slash my throat next?"

He remains silent as he stomps past me and up the stairs. About halfway to the next landing, he stops and says, "Ehrn–"

His next words are cut off by a deafening crack as another vampire bursts through the floor at the top of the steps, sending wood flying in all directions as he floats above us, blood and saliva dripping out of his mouth as he launches himself toward my partner. Khatazo wastes no time. He grabs the vampire by the neck and slams him into the steps. A horrifying crunch meets my ears the moment the vampire's spine connects with them, and just as the bloodthirsty creature lets out a pained howl, Khatazo lifts him over his head and slams the vampire's chest directly into the crown of sharp horns growing out of his skull. Perhaps even more effective than the wooden stake, Khatazo's horns instantly kill the vampire, and blood rains down on him like a waterfall.

He turns to face me, and I can barely tell where his eyes and nose are supposed to be with all the blood on his face. "I do not dazzle, Ehrn. That is not something I am capable of." Wrapping the ends of his hair around his hand, he squeezes some of the blood out before tossing his long locks back over his shoulder. Then he comes to meet me at the bottom of the steps and hurls me into his arms until he's carrying me like a princess. "And I will never hurt you. Never. I would sooner stop my own heart."

Stunned by the reverence in his voice, I remain quiet as he carries me past the hole in the floor the vampire popped out of, and it isn't until we reach the third landing that he puts me down.

There's no door on this landing, which confuses me. The only thing here is a small table with a half-melted tapered candle, and a rusty hammer lying next to it.

I pick up the hammer and examine it closely. "What are we supposed to do with this?"

The first step on the next landing explodes into kindling as another vampire launches into the air above us, fangs bared and ready to suck us dry. Khatazo rips the hammer from my hand and waits until the vampire is low enough, then slams it into the side of his head. That knocks the vamp to the floor. Khatazo hands the hammer back to me as the vampire crawls along the floor, dazed and trying to regain his strength. Khatazo grabs the vampire by his long blond ponytail and lifts his head enough to expose the vampire's throat. In a single motion, Khatazo sinks his fangs into the vampire's neck, and just as the wound starts spraying brown blood, the vampire explodes.

I let out a breath I didn't know I was holding as the hammer slips from my grasp and hits the floor with a clatter.

The noise cuts through the heavy silence, and the corner of Khatazo's mouth curls up in a lopsided grin. "Do you still wish to chat with these savages, or can I kill them the moment they appear so we can reach the end of this miserable staircase?"

Sighing, I reply, "Kill away, Big Red. This whack-a-vamp section of the track is officially my least favorite."

CHAPTER 7
KHATAZO

After three more floors and six dead vampires, we free ourselves from the wahk-a-vahmp staircase, as Ehrn called it, and discover a cleansing station on the ninth floor. Once Ehrn and I have washed the blood from our skin and changed into new uniforms, we find an unlocked door that has not one vampire lingering behind it. The room we enter doesn't have much occupying the space except for the many texts lining the shelves along the walls.

"Ooh, a library!" Ehrn cheers, clapping her hands together beneath her pointy chin. I find her constant elation puzzling. It irritated me when we first met, because it made her seem as if her brain was not working properly, but now I'm mystified by it. How can one encounter such darkness and still be this excited about anything? It does not make sense to me.

She starts pulling texts from the shelves, one at a time, and flipping through the pages.

"Can you read Crindan?" I ask, warily eyeing the bouquets of flowers between the books. There are several bouquets, and they seem to be purely decoration, but I do not trust any compound-grown flora after narrowly escaping the carnivorous plant room.

Ehrn puts a book back in its place, then grabs another. "For the most part," she says, chewing on the inside of her cheek. "Depending on when it was published. Old Crindan is really tricky though."

I grunt in agreement. "Too many extra vowels." Whenever I come across a text from centuries ago, I don't bother trying to read it. The old words confuse me.

"Yes," she adds enthusiastically, "and some of the verbs they used were insane. Like, *duufatakonorm?* What does that even mean?"

It feels as if a lightning bolt shoots straight into my cock. Why, of all the old Crindan words, did she have to pick that one to inquire about? "It is," I clear my throat, "a sexual act..."

"Oh," she mutters quietly as she returns the book to the shelf. Her head drops and she fidgets with her belt. "What, um, what is it exactly?"

"The planet Qontak. Have you heard of it?"

She nods.

I sigh and attempt to get the information out in a single breath. "Centuries ago, Qontak was used as a prison planet for rebels who fought against Motavvi rule. The prisoners were not permitted to leave their cells. Ever. In order to meet their sexual needs, they would..."

She looks at me expectantly, and I lose myself in the flecks of gold among the green of her eyes. "They would what?"

"Touch themselves while holding the gaze of another prisoner," I continue. "This was an invitation to participate. Once an invitation was accepted, the prisoners would engage in this act until release. It was an act of rebellion against those holding them captive," I finish, awkwardly rubbing a hand on the back of my neck. Now I cannot shake the image of Ehrn with her pants down and her legs spread wide as her fingers disappearing into the wet depths of her cunt.

Would she hold my gaze throughout? Would my name slip past her soft lips in a ragged moan?

My cock grows painfully hard the more I think about it.

"So it's like parallel play?" she asks. "Masturbating together?"

I had never heard it described as parallel play. "Yes," I begin, "though the traditional act of *duufatakonorm* would end with one laying beneath a spray of come from the other."

The redness of Ehrn's cheeks spreads down her neck, disappearing beneath her shirt. "I see," she says, her voice shaky.

"If there were multiple participants, the cells would get quite messy."

She chuckles, "I can see how that would piss off the guards."

Ehrn's palm flattens over her heart, and I wonder how rapidly it beats inside her chest. Is she feeling what I feel? The same desperation as me? The urge to remove our clothing right here in this room full of flowers and books and ravage each other until the walls crumble around us?

Her shoulders tremble, and I can see the tiny hairs on her forearm standing at attention. "You are cold?"

"Huh?" she asks, looking dazed. "Oh. Yeah, cold."

I notice a blanket folded neatly in a woven basket on a low shelf and hold it out to her.

Her fingers brush against mine as she takes it from me. The contact is electric, and I find myself unnerved by it, but also craving more.

"It's kinda nice in here," she notes, sitting down on the carpet and leaning her back against a shelf full of books. Her eyes flutter closed as she lets out a deep breath, looking relaxed.

When they open again, she pats the spot on the floor to her right. "Sit with me?"

"Have you finally grown tired of being frightened, Ehrn?"

I thought the day would never come. Ehrn has shown incredible stamina, along with maddening enthusiasm, for being in such a wretched place.

She pulls the blanket up over her shoulders. "No way. I think I'm just plain tired."

Ehrn's delicate features drop slightly, and I wonder where her mind has taken her to. My bones crack as I lower myself to a crouch. A grunt escapes me as I take my place at her side on the floor. She lifts the edge of the blanket and tosses half of it across my lap.

I'm not cold, but I have no intention of removing it, especially once Ehrn tucks it beneath my chin and leans her head against my shoulder.

Just as her breaths even out, the red fog enters the air, slowly filling the room and creating a billowing cloud. Ehrn coughs and we immediately duck beneath the safety of the thick fabric.

"What should we do?" she asks in a panic. "I didn't even look for a puzzle or the next door."

My heart races at her nearness, and I can't seem to look away from her lips. Her tongue traces along her bottom lip and her pupils dilate. I feel my sac tighten against my body, and I'm certain pre-come has begun to pool at my tip. This fog is only going to make it harder for me to remain next to her without touching her. I must extricate myself immediately.

"I will remain on the opposite wall until the fog passes," I tell her, getting onto my knees.

"Wait."

Ehrn puts a hand on my shoulder and squeezes, and I have to sink my fangs into the inside of my cheek to keep from coming. Her very touch has my entire body shaking. I ease back down next to her and give her a questioning glance.

One of her brows lifts. *"Duufatakonorm?"*

I bark out a laugh, certain she is making a joke of some kind. We are allies, not pleasure mates. Though I wouldn't object to adding this element to our partnership. My cock is so hard it's painful. The thicker the fog grows, the more desperate for her I will become, but that will inevitably make things between us more complicated. "You wish to...engage in..." I trail off. "Ehrn, I—"

She interrupts. "Why not?" Her gaze is determined as it drifts down my chest and lingers on my arms. "We know what the fog does, and I don't think we're getting out of here until it's gone. We won't touch each other. Only ourselves, okay? We deserve some relief." She points to the blanket still draped over our heads. "Besides, at least we have some privacy."

Ehrn lifts her hips and undoes her belt before slipping her hand beneath the waistband. Her green eyes never stray from mine as her hand starts to move.

It's only when I look down that I realize I've already begun stroking myself through my pants. My desire is consuming me, turning my mind to mush. She arches her back as the speed of her hand quickens. I hear the wetness of her cunt as her fingers slip through her folds.

I groan as I shove my pants down to my ankles and wrap my hand around my aching cock.

She sucks in a breath as she watches me stroke myself, and she wiggles her pants down past her knees. Her fingers glisten with her nectar as she resumes her position and focuses her attention on the pink, swollen bud at the crest of her folds.

Ehrn is so wet, her cunt dripping as spots cloud my vision. It takes the entirety of my restraint not to dip my head and shove my forked tongue into the depths of her heat. Saliva fills my mouth at the thought.

She moans and pinches her eyes shut as her fingers disappear inside her core. I'm mesmerized by the exquisiteness of this lush, frustrating female pleasuring herself with her hand. Her ample thighs shake as her movements grow erratic, and the silver stripes etched into the skin around her hips and inner thighs glow softly in the dim light.

My grip tightens around my cock as I thrust, wishing it was her hand in place of mine, or even better, her mouth. It gets hot beneath the blanket, but I would rather drown in my own sweat than rip the blanket off and reveal Ehrn's magnificent body to the empress and whomever else is stationed in front of the compound's cameras.

Ehrn's face contorts as her climax hits, and she lets out a loud, keening cry as she thrashes against the wall. She ends up shifting onto her back, her body boneless from the force of her orgasm. She reaches for the hem of her shirt and tugs it over her head, leaving her completely naked in front of me. A smirk tugs at her lips as her knees fall apart, and I get a clear, close look at the swollen lips of her cunt, soaking wet before me.

When she reaches down and traces along her seam, I lose control. I feel Ehrn's hand on my arm as she grips and moves me. I don't understand why until my seed is spurting all over her creamy stomach. She runs her hands through it and spreads it over her teats, the dark pink tips hardening beneath a layer of my come.

The sight fills me with a strange level of pride and something else. Something deep and unyielding. Something I fear will not release its grip on me anytime in the near future.

"More," she pleads, massaging my come into her skin. I give her what she wants, spraying across her lower stomach until my sac feels deflated.

I collapse against the wall, my chest heaving as I return to the present moment.

She giggles quietly as she takes in my disheveled state. "Did we do it right? *Duufatakonorm?*"

I nod. "I believe we did. Yes."

Better than anyone has ever done it before, I'd wager.

CHAPTER 8
ERIN

Khatazo offers me the blanket to clean up, and I wipe his sparkly lavender come off my chest and stomach before quickly throwing my uniform back on. Now that the fog has cleared, and we've both satisfied our needs, I feel much more energized to continue through the track. I also feel many other things that I'm not ready to address, mostly about how incredibly hot that parallel play session was, and how eager I am to do it again. I can't think about that right now though, because we need to keep moving.

Once we're dressed, Khatazo and I examine the bookshelves more closely. The bouquets of flowers are gorgeous, but seem strategically placed throughout the shelves like bookends, which I find odd. Why are there even this many flowers in here? Eight bouquets for one room? There's no furniture in here, but it looks far too orderly for the setting of a messy battle. A puzzle then, maybe? I can't find any puzzle pieces though, and there is no frame to put them in.

"I don't understand," Khatazo says, looking around with a discerning eye. Glad I'm not the only one who's confused.

"Let's see if we can just leave." I head toward the far door, but a low buzzing sound slowly builds until it's all I can hear. "What the f—"

I can't even finish dropping the f-bomb, and while I'm sure Granny would be pleased as punch by that, the swarm of bugs flying around my head is pissing me the fuck off. It's too dark in this room to get a good look at them, but from what I can see, they have large wings like dragonflies, four legs with pincers on the ends, and long white-and-brown-speckled bodies the size of my finger. That's a big-ass bug, and there are hundreds of them.

Khatazo shouts something at me, but I can't make out the words over the buzzing that's now deafening. "What?" I shout back.

"Run!" he yells. His big body bumps into me, pushing me toward what I hope is the door, and I close my eyes and cover my face with my hands as I put one foot in front of the other.

My elbows hit a wall, and I keep one hand over my eyes as I feel along the surface for a doorknob.

A sharp pinch at the back of my neck sends a painful jolt down my spine, and a bug crunches beneath my hand as I slap it. Triumph is quickly replaced by hot, blinding agony shooting down my body and into my fingertips. I let out a frustrated moan and drag my hip along the wall as I feel for the door, keeping both hands around my head.

"Over here!" Khatazo shouts. He doesn't sound far, and I stumble toward his concerned voice.

When I reach him, he pulls me into his arms and throws the door open, shoving me forward. My arms flail as I fall backward, and I snag his wrist, dragging him with me into a pool of water that fills the next room.

The moment I'm submerged, I notice this isn't normal water. It's thicker, with a brownish color and a syrupy texture, which can't be a good sign.

"Khatazo!" I yell when I breach the surface. I'm freaking out, which, as with the quicksand, is the last thing you're supposed to do. But this isn't regular water. Even if it were, it wouldn't matter. The result would be the same.

He wraps an arm around my waist and tugs me against him. "You're safe, Ehrn. I'm here."

I'm so grateful to hear his voice and feel his body against mine that tears stream down my face, making him look like a big red blur. "I-I can't swim," I choke out, the shame like weights tied to my ankles. "I d-don't know how."

He takes my hand and runs my fingers along the sharp protrusions near his elbow. "I have fins." Then he hauls me onto his back, wrapping my arms around his neck. "Don't let go."

I do as he says, holding as tightly as I can until he lets out what sounds like a cough mixed with a chuckle, signaling I need to loosen my grip a tad. My legs float behind me, but when I feel him start to kick through the water, I follow his lead, thinking it'll help us move faster.

He pops his head out of the water to say, "Stop. You're kicking *me*." So I cling to him like a barnacle on a ship as his arms and legs cut swiftly through the water.

A couple feet to our left, a spiked, serpent-like tail breaches the surface, and it splashes the sticky liquid at my face as my scream echoes off the walls. Some of the water gets into my mouth, and the mysterious acidic flavor will forever be burned into my memory. I never want to learn what it is or where it came from.

"Go! Go, go, go!" I shout, kicking my heel into Khatazo's ribs.

He looks up just as the tail pokes out of the water again, and he growls low in his throat before picking up the pace.

This pool is humongous, and even though we're already halfway across, it feels like we're standing still. We need to reach the other side before we learn exactly what that spiky-tailed creature is and how many of them are swimming around us.

Two more tails splash us from the other side, which means there are at least three serpents in here. The odds of us getting out of here alive go from bad to worse.

I kick Khatazo in the ribs again, even though I feel bad about it. I don't mean to treat him like a horse, but he really needs to swim faster. Like, now. Preferably *right* fucking now.

His body shifts to the side as if he's trying to swim around something, and my grip around his neck loosens, making me slide down his back. I let out several frustrated huffs as I wiggle my way back into place.

Just a few more strokes, and we'll make it to the other side, right in front of the door. My breath is lodged in my throat as I watch the distance between us and the ledge slowly disappear.

Suddenly, something latches onto my foot. I assume it's the serpent, and that theory is confirmed when I feel it move up my foot and past the top of my boot. Several large teeth sink into my lower calf, and I let go of Khatazo's neck the moment the fangs hit bone. I don't know if I scream, but I do know I've never felt pain like this before.

The serpent drags me beneath the surface of the water, and I wave my hands wildly, trying to fight its vise-like grip, but it's no use. I hold my breath as long as I can—which isn't very long—before the thick, sticky water floods my mouth, filling my lungs as the pain grows more intense. It feels like my blood is on fire and my bones are disintegrating.

Even my fingers and toenails hurt. How is that possible?

This is not how I want to die, but as the serpent drags me deeper and my vision starts to fade, I resign myself to my fate. I wonder how close we were to the finish line. To my fresh start. I guess I'll never know.

Before I lose consciousness, I feel the serpent's grip on my calf tighten then release me entirely, and I'm yanked above the surface as Khatazo tosses me over his shoulder and climbs out of the pool. He slaps my back over and over until I vomit, the brown water splattering all over the floor and burning the bejesus out of my throat and sinuses in the process.

I don't even notice the massive open wounds on my leg until Khatazo curses under his breath.

"Oh," I mutter between coughs. My leg tingles, and the rest of me is somehow sweating *and* shivering, but I can't feel anything beyond that. I must be in shock because several silver-dollar-sized holes gouge my leg, and I'm not even screaming. I should be screaming.

"Can you walk?" Khatazo asks, his yellow eyes filled with what I am sure is worry, his thin, vertical pupils widening slightly the longer he looks at my leg.

A loud cackle fills through the room, and it takes me a minute to realize it's coming from me. Though it was a rather silly question. "Can I walk?" I repeat before throwing my head back and laughing some more. "I'm fairly certain my leg will need to be amputated, so walking is out of the question."

He looks around the room for first aid supplies, I assume, but there are none in here. What he does next catches me by surprise.

Khatazo stares at the inside of his forearm, then lowers his head and rips a gash in the skin with his fangs, creating a large open cut where his black blood instantly begins to pool. He turns his arm over and lets the blood drip into my wounds.

"Wh—hey! What are you doing?" I shriek, trying to scoot away from him. There's no way this will help, and at the very least, it's extremely unsanitary.

"You will survive," he says quietly. Then, louder, "Do you hear me? You must survive."

The tingling sensation in my leg fades and is quickly replaced by a sting so sharp that my eyes water, and I have to bite my sleeve to keep from crying.

"The Bugoros conquered my home planet and enslaved my people," he explains, his words a welcome distraction from the agony. "They found our blood has healing properties. Household servants were required to give blood each moon cycle to ensure the health of the king and political leaders."

He grunts as he squeezes his arm, causing more blood to spill from the cut he gave himself. When his gaze meets mine, my body warms, and I wonder if the fog is lingering in my system. "I don't know if my blood can heal humans," he says, swallowing hard, "but you must live, Ehrn. I can't do this without you."

CHAPTER 9
KHATAZO

I fill the silence in the pool room with mindless chatter as I wait to see if my blood helps heal Ehrn's wounds. We remain on the edge of the pool, a safe distance from the choppy, serpent-infested waters, as I watch over her. The punctures on her leg are deep, and even if we had access to medical supplies, I'm not sure they would be enough to undo the damage the serpent has caused.

Fiyking serpents. Three of them splash the revolting brown liquid at us as they pass by, probably in anger because they cannot reach us here. I would laugh at their pettiness if I weren't so worried about Ehrn. I'm not leaving the compound without her. Even if I must carry her lifeless body through a dozen more rooms while fighting an army of twisted beasts, I will do so, if only to ensure her remains are properly cared for.

My entire body trembles at the thought of losing her. It's an entirely unacceptable outcome. She's not mine, I know this, but she deserves to live a full life exactly as she has imagined it—with her tiny house and tiny garden and endless quiet.

It sounds boring and dreadful, but if it's what Ehrn wants, then she should have it.

She asks me questions about the Bugoros, and I answer each. None of the memories are pleasant, but Ehrn listens intently and squeezes my hand when my voice grows thick with emotion.

I tell her about Aukellin and Qibor, and the time we ended up with a bag full of fake *skzanit* rubies and Qibor's torn-up arm.

"Not our finest performance," I say, embarrassed at how easily we were swindled.

"Don't beat yourself up," Ehrn says warmly. "My college boyfriend bought me these gorgeous diamond earrings—well, he *said* they were diamonds—but they were actually cubic zirconia, and even when I put them next to real diamonds, I still couldn't tell the difference."

I find myself staring at her, lost completely in her gaze. To have her focused attention, this female who found me sobbing in a hallway and dragged me to safety, it feels like a gift. A gift I'm not sure I'm worthy of receiving.

"Tell me more about them," she demands. "Your crew."

I tip my head back as happy memories flood my mind. "Aukellin is my brother. He is the most charming among us and the females we've encountered seem to agree. They find him nice to look at, I think."

Her furry brow lifts. "Ooh, so he's the pretty one?"

"I suppose he is, yes. He is the one who dazzles," I add, finding it pointless to disagree. "When a job requires an easy smile, we send him in first. When brute force is preferred, I go in first."

"And what about the other guy?"

"Qibor," I clarify. How to describe Qibor? "Qibor has felt like a brother for most of my life. Our mothers were close, and he has always been there. I have no memories that don't prominently feature him. But he is different."

"How so?"

"He exists mostly inside his own mind. It's a brilliant mind. We have yet to encounter a problem that Qibor can't solve, but he rarely speaks. I understand the language of his grunts, but I imagine to someone who doesn't know him, he might seem strange and distant. The Bugoros would often beat him for being too quiet."

Ehrn's face twists with disgust. "That's awful. My sister was like that. Teachers always scolded her for not participating enough in class or not wanting to read in front of everyone. One teacher even told our mom that there was something wrong with her. Some people only speak when they have something meaningful to contribute, and there's nothing wrong with that."

"Yes, you understand," I reply, finding comfort in knowing there are others like him. I received more than one lashing from the Bugoros for defending Qibor. The fury of seeing him tortured for being who he was is still fresh. Aukellin and I would be long dead without that methodical mind of his. "When we discovered the rubies were fake on that last job, my temper got us in trouble. I wanted to decapitate the *fiyking* crooks who set us up, and Qibor tried to stop me. It was a crowded market, and chaos erupted because of the shots I fired. The weapons they had..." I trail off, wincing as I relive the event. "They were different from ours. More advanced. The bullets were not bullets. They were canons that exploded upon finding their target. Qibor stepped in front of Aukellin, blocking the path of the canon, and had he not made that choice," I shudder, "Aukellin would be dead."

Ehrn laces her fingers through mine, the webbing between mine limiting her grip, but I squeeze back, grateful for the warmth in her touch. "That's why he needs a cybernetic implant?"

I nod. "He's lucky his arm was the only part of him we couldn't save. There are burns that cover his chest and stomach, but he doesn't care about that. His only complaint since it happened is that he is unable to work at full capacity with only one arm."

"I'd love to meet him," she says with a smile. It's the first time either of us has mentioned what comes after we leave the compound. We seem to notice it in the same moment, and she rushes to change the subject.

She tells me stories about her home, somewhere called Jee-or-jah, located on planet Uurth, and while I do not understand most of the words she uses, the way she smiles with her whole face warms my insides.

I tell her more about the empress and the reign of terror the Motavvi family has inflicted on the people across the Crinda Galaxy for centuries.

"Hey," she exclaims, pointing at her foot. "I can wiggle my toes."

I did not realize she was incapable of doing that before, but I am relieved that my blood seems to be working. "Good. That is good." She tries to get up at one point, but I gently nudge her down onto her back. "There is no rush. We do not have a time limit to complete the track. Take your time. We'll move when your body is ready."

Ehrn argues at first, but ultimately lies back.

She tells me more about her sister, and how they both went to live with their grahn-nee in the South when their mother died from an accidental drug overdose. "That was a tough time," she says, her tone somber but never wavering. "My sister was ten. She didn't really understand what happened, but I did." Ehrn laughs to herself.

"Granny didn't go easy on us. She started whipping us into shape on the ride to Georgia from Mom's funeral. We learned the proper way to eat soup, which forks to use for salad, and if we ever swore in front of her," Ehrn throws her head back with a huff, "whew, boy. That automatically meant no dinner and thirty minutes of sucking on a bar of soap."

"Soap?" I ask, unsure if I understand her meaning. "What would that solve?"

"Cleaning out a dirty mouth." She nods when I give her a horrified look. "You only make that mistake once."

The words tumble out of my mouth as soon as they enter my head. "You are much hardier than you appear."

Ehrn stares at me for a moment, and I wonder if I have insulted her. Then her green eyes sparkle with amusement, and a smile tugs at the corners of her lips as she says, "Thank you. I love when others underestimate me."

"You do?"

"Oh yeah. It's my favorite thing."

I chuckle at her response. "Why is that?"

She props herself up on her elbows. "Because there's nothing more satisfying than witnessing the moment someone realizes they were wrong about you. It's just..." She trails off, scrunching her little nose as her gaze lifts to the ceiling. It's like she has to mush her features together to find the correct words she seeks, and I find it adorable. "So delicious. If I could bottle that feeling, I'd drink it by the gallon."

I'm growing attached to this female, and that's a problem I don't know how to solve. If we make it out of here, we'll each collect our credits, and she will waste all of hers traveling to Yeronix for a quiet life she will never have. Empress Motavvi is luring her and those like her to that planet under the guise of safety and prosperity, but I would bet my life that neither can be found there.

Part of me is angered by Ehrn's ignorance. She's smarter and stronger than she looks, but this is a trap she is strolling directly into. We have endured so much together. I feel obligated to keep her safe. No, not obligated, precisely. That's not the right word. I feel it's my duty, but also an honor. I want to protect her for as long as she'll let me.

"Ooh, check me out," Ehrn says with a wide grin. She rotates her foot in a circle, then goes in the opposite direction. "I think I might be able to stand on it."

Before she can shift onto her hands and knees, I put a hand on her shoulder. "Not yet."

I use my claws to tear the leg of my pants below the knee and rip that cloth into three strips. Putting pressure on the wounds, I wrap the cloth strips around them and tie a secure knot against her shin. The bleeding has stopped, which is a good sign, but I'm still not sure Ehrn should be putting weight on it.

Slowly, she pulls herself forward, and I insist she leans on me as she rises. It takes a while, especially with my repeated insistence that she not rush, but she does stand. She's not fully healed and leans heavily against my side as she limps across the floor, but it is a far better outcome than I first envisioned.

It's not until we're standing in front of the door that we realize there's a circular puzzle above the handle that we need to solve in order to unlock it. The pieces hang in a small sack beneath the knob, and Ehrn opens it into her palm to study the pieces.

"There are so many of these," she says with a frown. "And they're all the same color."

"Let me see," I say, pretending to examine the puzzle pieces. "Ah, yes." I look closely at the frame on the door, take a deep inhale, and shove my fist into the center of the frame. The mechanism that unlocks the door is crushed beyond recognition, but when I hear a click below the knob, the door opens.

Ehrn giggles, the sound echoing through the room and making my heart skip. "Well done, sir."

I help her hobble into the next room, the smallest by far, and we scan the walls for clues as to what we can expect.

"Just a bunch of levers," she says, sounding equally confused and wary. It's how I've felt most of the time I've been in the compound, and I'm pleased to finally hear some skepticism coming from her.

"Shall we pull?" I ask.

"Think the door is unlocked and we can just leave without touching anything?"

I shake my head. "Unlikely," I reply. But I indulge her in case she is right. We make it to the door; the knob doesn't turn. I slam my fist into the center of it, but not even a dent is left behind. It's the sturdiest door we have faced.

It's frustrating to offer Ehrn my strength and have it not be enough to deliver results, but once again, we shall rely on Ehrn's resilient spirit until we may exit this room.

She sighs heavily. "Let's pull, I guess."

We slowly make our way around the room, first pulling on one lever and waiting for the torment to come. When nothing happens, we move on to the next, and the next, and the next, until there's only one lever left. Ehrn pulls on it, and her grip on my back tightens as we wait.

The monsters never arrive, but what does come is the red fog.

We exchange a knowing glance as it fills the room, and I lower myself to the ground to wait it out. She drops into my lap and leans her head against my shoulder. My fingers flex with the desperate urge to touch her, to caress her soft skin and unpeel the layers of her clothing until she's lying bare before me. I resist though, because giving in to my needs would mean disregarding hers, and that is unthinkable. I won't do it.

"We shall wait," I vow. "The fog will dissipate, and we'll leave."

I shift Ehrn in my lap, hoping she cannot feel the erection barely concealed by my pants. Her hot breath fans my chest, and the world stops moving. The moons, the suns, the planets that fill each galaxy across the universe—none of it matters. Everything outside this room ceases to exist in this moment with her skin against mine. She places her palm on my stomach, and I grit my teeth the moment it starts to move lower.

Covering her hand with mine, I growl, "Stop."

She looks up at me, her beautiful eyes swirling with lust, and I am powerless. It's then that I realize this little human has my heart, and she's not even aware of it. "Why? You don't like when I touch you?"

I hold her gaze, for the first time noticing the lines that spread from the corners of her eyes and hug the outer edges of her delicate mouth. So very captivating. "I like it far too much, Ehrn. This is the problem."

Her lips part at my words, and I wonder if the rapid heartbeat I hear is coming from her chest or mine.

The fog does eventually dissipate, but when we try the knob, it remains locked. We return to our spot on the floor, and this time, Ehrn sits beside me. She wraps her arm through mine and her fingers lightly squeeze my bicep.

"Now what?" she asks.

"I don't know."

A moment later, the fog returns, this time thicker and more potent than the last.

Ehrn places her hands on either side of my face and pulls me closer.

I grab her wrists. "No, Ehrn."

"You don't want me?"

I can hear the hurt in her tone, and it's the last thing I want her to feel. "No," I tell her with a groan. "I want you more—"

My words are cut off by the soft press of her lips against mine. At first, I'm frozen, unsure if I should proceed. I know if I kiss her back, I will never want to stop. When the smooth tip of her tongue brushes against the seam of my lips, my chest burns with longing, and I lose all semblance of control. My fingers get lost in the long strands of her mane as I savor the taste of her.

Her lips slide across mine in a way that feels like a caress, but her tongue is hot and determined as it pushes past my lips. I suck on her tongue, pulling it into my mouth and letting the forked end of mine dance around hers.

Then she pulls back, her pupils blown out as she looks at me. "I need this," she says in a breathy moan that goes straight to my cock. "I need you, Khatazo."

"You're certain?" I ask, terrified knowing I've just given her a way out. I need her more than I need my next breath, but I won't pressure her into this.

"Yes," she says, pressing her forehead against mine. "Touch me. Please."

Her words release something inside me, and a growl rips from my throat as I gently toss her onto her back. I look down at her clothes with anger. How dare they come between my eyes and her magnificent skin? I tear them from her body and toss them across the room.

A word pops into my head at the sight of her naked. Only one word, and the longer I look at her, the deeper it sinks into my soul: *Mine.*

CHAPTER 10

ERIN

I expect Khatazo to devour me like a man starved the second I'm naked, but he doesn't. His gaze travels down my body slowly, so slowly, I grow uncomfortable under such focused attention, but he sucks in a breath and places a hand over his heart. "You are no human. You are a goddess." He moves backward on his knees and bends down, pressing his forehead into the tips of my toes.

"What are you doing?"

He looks up at me through his long white eyelashes. "I'm worshiping at your feet of course."

I giggle shyly. "Duh."

Khatazo presses a featherlight kiss to each toe, then along my shins—carefully avoiding the bandaged area—and then moves up my knees and thighs. For someone whose lungs are filled with the sex fog, he sure is taking his time to savor me.

I don't think I have the patience for that though. Not this time anyway. My pussy clenches around nothing and my clit pulses with need. I don't even need to touch myself to know I'm wet. Just looking at Khatazo with his strong jaw, intense reptilian gaze, and muscled, heaving chest has me rolling my hips, trying to close the distance between our bodies.

I could stare at him for days and never tire of the view. Suddenly, little details I never noticed before, or didn't have the capacity to notice with the horrors of the compound closing in on us, become clear as day. There are glowing, thin white lines—I assume they're tattoos—that start on the outside of his nostrils, trace the outside of his wide, rugged nose, and jut out above his brows. They're so subtle, they remind me of wrinkles, but up close, it's clear they're so much more interesting than that.

"Touch me," I beg, my hand going to my breast and squeezing.

He groans as he watches me stroke and pluck at my nipple until it pebbles. "Mine," he breathes, his voice a low, velvety purr.

The fog is starting to dissipate again, but my need for him pulses through my bones, and I suspect that the strange red mist is playing a smaller role than I originally thought. Sure, I might not have gotten naked in the compound without it, especially given that there are cameras everywhere—the knowledge of which is only making me wetter—but I found Khatazo attractive before the fog first emerged. My desire for him has only grown stronger ever since.

And it's not just desire. With each brush of his hand against mine, his promises to keep me safe—which he immediately made good on by killing any creature who came near me—and most importantly, the way he made himself bleed in the unlikely chance that his blood could heal me, the pull I've felt toward him continues to intensify.

The fog is not influencing me to have sex with him, it's just bringing me to the same inevitable conclusion I'd have gotten to eventually without it. "I want this," I tell him, needing to say the words aloud so he knows how present I am.

In a brief moment of clarity, I remember that, thankfully, Gr'va helped me find drinkable birth control that works on humans at the station a few weeks ago, so I won't need to worry about getting knocked up by a rogue alien pirate.

Khatazo removes his belt, tossing it aside, and roughly shoves his pants down his legs before kicking them off. His huge, glorious cock springs free, and I'm pretty sure I utter, "Holy fucking shit."

Sorry, Granny! Though I suppose some things are worth sucking on soap for.

I saw it in the library, but those were different circumstances. He wasn't about to rearrange my organs with it. "I'm not sure you'll fit," I tell him, reaching out and taking him in my hand. He's hard, obviously, but it's not just that he's erect; his dick is like a red pole made of smooth granite. But unlike a cool exterior of stone, he's hotter here than the rest of his body, and I shudder when he starts pumping into my grip.

The moment his hips start to move, little dark slits appear down his length and curved maroon ridges appear, tickling my palm.

"You will take me, Ehrn," he says, panting. "All of me."

I nod as I guide his dick toward my entrance, powerless to suggest otherwise when he's looking at me with such ardent possessiveness. Running the tip along the seam of my pussy, Khatazo's entire body begins to tremble. When he removes my hand, I let out a pitiful whine.

"I must ensure you're ready first," he says, cupping my mound and easily slipping two fingers inside.

A couple thrusts of his hand are all it takes before wet sounds fill the room, and he smiles proudly, his forked tongue peeking out between his lips just enough to remind me of how exquisite that kiss was earlier. Forked tongues are the best tongues. This is an indisputable fact.

"Mmm," he groans, his eyes falling closed. "So wet for me, little Ehrn."

Never in my entire life have I been described as little, but compared to Khatazo, I suppose I am.

I part my thighs as wide as they'll go and press my nails into his back, pulling him closer. "Now, Khatazo. Need you now." My pussy is dripping and so ready to be filled, I can barely see straight.

He gives in to my demands, slowly pushing his hard cock through my swollen folds. His back and shoulders are rigid as he enters my core, his face scrunched in agony as he holds himself back, clearly restraining himself to ensure my comfort. "Tell me if I hurt you."

"No pain," I tell him, giving his thick forearm a reassuring squeeze. My vocabulary becomes more limited the deeper he goes, those incredible ridges touching me in places I never knew existed. "So good."

After what feels like a century of waiting, our hips meet and he's fully sheathed inside me. I can't move. I can't breathe. The only thing I can do is feel. And I feel him everywhere.

"I'm going to move," he warns through gritted teeth, his jaw flexing as his control wanes.

I nod. His heavy balls hang against my ass, and I've never felt so full. Then he pulls almost all the way out before slamming back into me, and stars dance behind my eyelids as I hold on for dear life. My entire body is shaking beneath him, and I don't notice it until he sets a brutal pace, but then I feel it. His ridges...they're vibrating.

"Oh god," I cry out, slamming my head back on the floor. Every nerve in my body comes alive and heat pools low in my belly, telling me my orgasm is already starting to build. Not surprising, considering I'm stuffed to the gills with a gigantic cock and a dozen vibrating ridges.

He wraps a hand around my neck, gripping my nape. "Look at me," he growls.

Forcing my eyes open, I focus on the yellows of his irises to ground me.

"Mine," he says again. I don't disagree. I'm his in all ways right now, and I don't want that to change. Eventually it will, once we reach the finish line and go our separate ways, but right now, I'm his and he's mine, and there's nothing else but us.

My breasts bounce each time he drives into me, and he watches intently, groaning after every jiggle. He drops his head and swipes the forked tip of his tongue across my nipple, and the orgasm that's been building tears up my spine suddenly, violently, and explodes out of me.

The roll of my hips turns erratic as my walls clench around him. Khatazo's thrusts continue, and when I come again, I feel myself floating through space and time, no longer tied to a physical body, but taking on a completely new form that is pure sensation. I shake and float and come while he roars into the sky and his hot seed fills me.

He growls into the crook of my neck, and his heavy body collapses on top of me. I expect to feel crushed, for my ribs to actually crack under his weight, but it feels good to be under him like this. His body covers mine so well that I practically disappear beneath him, and right here, I've never felt safer.

He whispers words of tenderness in my ear as he peppers my cheek and neck with kisses, and I rub his back. "Is it always like this?" he asks, his forked tongue tracing the shell of my ear. "I have had other partners, but this felt–"

"No," I tell him reverently. "This," I sigh, "this is rare."

He grunts in response, and I wish I could hear his thoughts.

We take our time getting dressed, and when we try to turn the knob this time, the door opens. "Well, I'll be damned. I guess the empress wanted a show." I look up at one of the cameras in the corner of the ceiling, put on my brightest smile, and bow. "You're welcome."

I never expected to enjoy the feeling of being watched, but knowing people could see me as Khatazo gave me the best orgasms of my life is surprisingly hot. If we weren't already dressed, I'd suggest we do it again.

Khatazo chuckles as he takes my hand and guides me through the door. The pad of my thumb runs along the delicate edges of the webbing between his fingers, learning the differences between my body and his. As soon as the door shuts, four steel cages in the room we're in fly open, and the biggest, freakiest wolves I've ever seen crawl out. Their fur is an off-white, beige color, their eyes are blood-red and bulge out of their sockets as if on the verge of popping like balloons, long gray feathers encircle their necks, and they walk on six legs.

Maybe I'm still dazed by the incredible sex, but an idea forms in my head that I just can't shake. Taking a cautious step forward, I say, "Granny had a dog that was always in a bad mood, but I was the only one who could get on his good side." I reach out a hand. "If I just—"

"No, Ehrn!" Khatazo shouts, yanking me back behind him.

The volume and aggression of his voice frighten the space-wolves, and they yip and howl while digging at the floor, as if kicking up dirt.

"You need to speak in a baby voice," I point out. "Dogs like that."

"These are not Uurth dogs," he says, bungling the name of my home planet like he has my name. "Stay behind me."

I don't listen. I know I should, but I can't help but peek around his bicep to look at them one more time, if only to remind myself that these are dangerous creatures who want to kill me. One of them catches me peeking, and white foam flies out of its mouth as its jaw snaps shut.

"Are you a fool?" Khatazo asks, his tone harsh and mocking. "Letting you get mauled by these beasts is not something I will allow. I've witnessed enough death for one lifetime. You wouldn't understand."

It's the worst possible time to get into this discussion, with the snarling, feathered spider-wolves closing in on us, but I feel the need to set the record straight. "Actually, I do know that pain. I know it very well. You know my mom died, but my sister died too. In a hospital bed, two years after she was diagnosed with a brain tumor."

Khatazo's hands drop to his sides as he listens, still facing away from me and toward the wolves.

"Granny had a heart attack in the kitchen as we were baking muffins," I continue. "Everyone I've loved has not only died, but they died in front of me. So don't talk to me like I'm some help-less little lamb."

His head drops, and he lets out a frustrated growl as he scrubs a hand down his face. "I'm sorry, Ehrn. You're not a help-less layy-umb. I didn't mean that."

My eyes roll at the adorable way he pronounces lamb, and it eases some of my anger.

"Allow me to rid us of these creatures, and I shall fill the hole I've made in our alliance, yes?"

"Okay, fine," I say with a chuckle, knowing he's sincere, and that his promise to *fill the hole* is probably an unintended sexual innuendo.

I make myself as small as possible behind Khatazo's back as their growls get louder. He growls back, and I press my forehead against the wall as the fighting begins.

It doesn't take long for him to obliterate the small pack, and

I turn just as he kicks a limp body toward the ceiling. The force of it cracks one of the ceiling panels in half, and the broken pieces fall to the floor, covering some of the mess.

I laugh at the ridiculousness of it all, but Khatazo puts a finger to his lips and points to the hole in the ceiling. That's when I hear it. People talking. Two women, by the sound of it.

"The empress," Khatazo whispers.

Stepping over a severed head, I get closer to the hole, and their words become clear.

"I will say it was an unexplained weather event," the empress says, her tone casual.

"You think they will believe this explanation?" the other person, Doctor S'Ko, I think, asks.

The empress laughs. "Have you seen some of the beings that come to settle on Yeronix? They have the weakest bodies and smallest brains in the galaxy. They will not question it."

Okay. Not loving the direction this conversation is taking so far.

"But has Yeronix ever had a red fog like this?" Doctor S'Ko asks. "Historically, the fog on the planet has been a light purple shade, has it not?"

Oh my god. The empress wants to release the sex fog on the residents of Yeronix? Why?

The empress sighs impatiently. "Even with the open borders, my subjects are not breeding at the pace I need them to. The fog will fix that."

Sweet baby Jesus. She's going to drug an entire planet to get them to have sex. Entire races of people will be so high on the red fog that they'll have unprotected sex, get pregnant, and have children with people they don't know or care about.

I...I can't think or breathe. What does this mean for me? For the life I've been fantasizing about? The life I'm so close to achieving?

"We just need to acquire more of the humans," the empress adds. "In terms of gestation, they are the ideal breeders."

I race toward the door, and thankfully, it's unlocked. The next room is a sustenance station, and there's nobody else in here. The perfect place for me to curl into a ball and mourn my shattered dreams.

CHAPTER II
KHATAZO

I was right about Yeronix being a trap. Though I don't say this to Ehrn. She sobs in a ball on the floor of the sustenance station, and seeing her this heartbroken claws at my insides.

The empress is a vile creature, and this plan of hers does not surprise me in the least. She has selfish goals, and she pursues them thoughtlessly. It's the way she has always been, much like her father before her and her grandmother before him. The Motavvis are a political dynasty, and many have lost their lives under Motavvi rule.

I don't know how to comfort Ehrn at this moment. She wants stability, quiet, and a place to call her own. That image of her life has been destroyed. I'm glad she is able to see the empress for who she truly is, but I didn't want it to be like this.

Ehrn doesn't let me hold her while she cries. It's the only thing I wish to do, but I respect that she doesn't want it right now. She doesn't eat anything while at the sustenance station. I consume three protein cubes and two bags of water. When I offer her a bite, she shakes her head, her shoulders sagging and her head low.

We move on to the next room, which has four puzzles. Ehrn remains quiet as she gathers the pieces and puts them into the frames on the wall. I offer to help, but she dismisses me, half-heartedly moving about the room and not even cracking a smile after each one is solved.

The door unlocks after the fourth puzzle is complete, and the finish line appears before us. Empress Motavvi and Doctor S'Ko stand side by side and cheer in applause as we step across the line. The trio of tiny creatures who placed the circular discs all over my body quickly remove them from my skin, then do the same for Ehrn before returning our personal items to us.

"On behalf of Crinda, I would like to thank you both for your participation in our study. The data you've allowed us to gather will be used to create groundbreaking advances in Crindan medicine," Empress Motavvi says, her tone sickly sweet as she pretends to be grateful for the hell we just endured. Her soul is full of rot and her false smile and fake gratitude mean nothing. She cares naught for benefiting anyone except herself. She might fool others, but she doesn't fool me.

She steps in front of Ehrn and takes one of her hands. I grit my teeth at the sight, trying to resist the urge to tear the skin off her face for touching what is mine.

"I must say, human," she begins, not even attempting to use Ehrn's name, "your performance in the compound was quite impressive. In fact, I would like to offer you a residence on the neighboring planet of Yeronix. Have you heard of it?"

The furry lines above Ehrn's eyes lift at the offer, and I silently beg for her to turn it down.

"Yes," Ehrn says, clearing her throat. "I have."

"It's a beautiful planet, full of beings like you who want a place to call their own."

Diabolical.

"In addition to the credits from this study," the empress

continues, "I would like to reward you with a two-bedroom home on the south corner of Yeronix, free of charge."

"That is quite a generous offer," Doctor S'Ko exclaims with wide eyes, as if they have not practiced spewing this lie a dozen times. "What say you, human?"

"Um…" Ehrn trails off.

No, no, no, Ehrn. Do not fall for this.

I want to shout the words at the top of my lungs, but the empress would surely have me hanged for such an affront to her generosity, fake though it may be.

As surprised as I am to see Ehrn contemplate this, I'm more surprised by her restraint. This is the same empress that crushed her dreams two rooms ago. While she views her problems through a lens made of sunshine, Ehrn could not possibly be considering accepting this offer from the empress. Could she?

"Thank you," Ehrn finally replies. "It's a lot to consider. I'll think about it."

She will think about it? Why? What is there to think about? She either chooses a life without freedom as a breeder on Yeronix, fornicating with males who care nothing for her, or she makes a different choice. Perhaps with me.

I can't offer a stable life of quiet like she wants, but I would put my energy into making her smile. I'd put her needs before my own, and I would spend each night using my fingers, tongue, and cock to give her the pleasure she deserves.

I may not be the mate she has long envisioned, or even the mate she wants, but I would give anything to keep her.

CHAPTER 12

ERIN

Empress Motavvi instructed us to make our way into the garden at the back of the compound while I consider her offer. It's dark out, probably the middle of the night if I had to guess, and the air is crisp and refreshing as it hits my skin. Tall, slender robots wheel around the grass, holding trays of finger sandwiches and chilled glasses of *wispo*.

I decline each time they roll past me because my appetite is nonexistent. It's not because of the empress's offer. I already know my answer to that will be a polite—but firm—no, thank you. There's no way in heck I'd willingly move to Yeronix after learning about the fog and how she intends to use it.

The thing that's messing with me is why Khatazo hasn't invited me to go with him on his ship. I know we agreed to be allies inside the compound, never promising anything beyond that, but I thought we had a real connection. I feel closer to him than I've ever felt with anyone. We survived some serious situations and remained a steadfast team throughout the track.

Maybe these feelings are one-sided though. He said I was his, but that could've been passionate sex talk, not meant to be taken seriously.

And I know he doesn't owe me anything, so maybe it's unreasonable for me to hope he'll want to continue whatever this is between us.

I sigh as I drop my head in my hands. Where do I go from here? Back to the station? Spend the rest of my days working at The Meat Pocket, stinking to high heaven of grease? That sounds miserable. Though the credits I've earned will certainly make life more comfortable, without knowing where it's safe to settle, I'd probably just stay at the station and move into a bigger apartment that I wouldn't have to share with anyone. I might get more space, but I still wouldn't be able to wander around the station on my own, and without Gr'va, I'd get lonely too. I don't want any of that.

Empress Motavvi's eyes light up when she exits the back gates and spots us on a bench in the middle of the garden. "There you are." Instinctively, I get to my feet and bow my head when she comes to stand in front of me. "Have you decided yet?" she asks, her mouth forming a tight line as she takes me in. I'm sure she's not used to waiting for anything. This must be infuriating for her.

Too bad.

"Indeed," I say, steeling my spine. I'm not about to be intimidated by this evil wretch, no matter how elegant she looks while committing unspeakable acts of cruelty. "Thanks for the offer, ma'am, but I'm gonna pass."

"You wish to pass?" she asks, her voice going up an octave. "On free lodgings on a peaceful planet?"

"Yep," I reply, crossing my arms. I refuse to give her an explanation because she doesn't deserve one. Also, it doesn't matter. She won't care what I think about her plans to use the fog. I'm nothing to her. She didn't even bother to learn my name.

She clears her throat. "That is a shame. Best of luck in the few remaining years your body has left in this life." She stomps back through the gates and into the compound. I hope I never have to see her sharp, angular face again.

Khatazo is grinning like a possum eating a sweet potato when I turn to face him. "Excellent decision," he says, nodding with pride.

We walk through the exit and into the night air, our watches buzzing the moment the credits hit our accounts, saying nothing as we make our way toward the port.

"Do you wish to return to the station?" he asks.

No, I almost say. *I want to stay with you. Invite me to stay with you. Don't let me go.*

"I can give you a ride on my ship, if you would like."

"Oh," I reply, my lip wobbling with emotion I don't want him to see. "Okay, yeah. Thanks."

I could swear I hear him growl quietly in response, but I have no idea why. If he didn't want to take me to the station, why offer?

Whatever. He gets to take his credits, get his buddy all patched up, and return to a life of treasure hunting while I spend hours picking through globs of meat for spoiled, moldy pieces to throw away.

On the way to his ship, we pass the shuttle stop I used to get here. A long line of people wait to board, and I wonder how many of them are dreading going back to their lives in spite of the credits earned here. What kinds of horrors did they encounter in the compound that will continue to haunt their dreams? For me, it's gotta be the sea-serpents. Or maybe the giant bugs. Or the quicksand. Lots of trauma is coming back to the station with me, and there'll be plenty of time to unpack it.

"Which ship is yours?" I ask as we near the end of a row of impressively large and shiny ships.

The sound of metal crumpling beneath Khatazo's fist makes me jump. The roar that follows sends shivers down my spine.

"Am I not worthy of being your mate?" he shouts, twisting the mangled remains of a streetlamp in his grip. "Is it because of the ghost hallway? The way I wept in front of you?"

"Whoa, what?" I ask, utterly confused. "What are you talking about?"

"Or is it the puzzles? You require a mate skilled at puzzle-solving? I can do that. Or I can *try* to be better at it. Perhaps there is training I can ta—"

"Hey," I say in a soft voice, holding out my hands like I would if I spotted a skittish deer in the woods. "It's okay." When the murderous look in his eyes starts to fade, I say, "I don't care if you're good at puzzles. Why would that bother me?"

He tosses the crushed metal aside and crosses his arms. "Ehrn, I know I'm not your ideal mate, but you're mine, and I would like to keep you."

He wants to keep me? As in forever?

The deeper the words sink in, the wider my smile gets. Khatazo wants to make me his mate, move me onto his ship, and spend his life by my side. My heart is so full, I'm worried it's about to burst. "Interesting," I say, taking a step closer to him. "Because I thought I annoyed you."

"You do!" he shouts. "You are far too positive, especially when optimism is inappropriate. I worry you will wander into the mouth of a *rom tuk qi* beast simply because you think his tongue is pretty."

I laugh because he's not wrong. Of course I'd want to get a closer look at a *rom tuk qi* beast with a pretty tongue, whatever that is, but I wouldn't be stupid enough to let it eat me, and though he's shouting otherwise, I think he knows that too.

He steps toward me, keeping me locked in his gaze. "But

even in the darkest corners of that miserable compound, you found the light. You...*are* the light."

My heart skips several beats. He's giving me exactly what I want wrapped in the most beautiful words I've ever heard. So why does he still seem so distraught?

"I fear my soul has grown too dark to see that light without you, Ehrn." He sighs, turning his back to me. "I wish you felt the same."

I launch myself at him like a flying squirrel and wrap my arms and legs around him the moment I land on his back. "I do feel the same, you big red dummy."

"What?" he says, jerking his head around to look at me.

I slide down his body and hop around him until we're face to face. "I don't want to go back to the station. That place sucks. My life there sucks. I want you and everything you have to offer."

Khatazo searches my face as if trying to uncover a lie.

"I never said you weren't good enough for me," I tell him, pressing the point of my chin into his chest as I gaze up at him. "That wasn't even a thought that entered my mind. I like you the way you are. You didn't invite me to stay with you on your ship, so I figured you didn't want me. And I wasn't about to invite myself. Granny taught me better than that."

"You will stay with me?" he asks, his deep voice cracking with hope. "I can't give you the quiet life you wished for on Yeronix, but I will give you the protection of my body, and the stability you seek can be found in my heart, which is eternally yours."

I smile up at him, joy seeping out of my every pore. "That's more than enough for me."

He lifts me into his arms as if I weigh nothing, and I cross my feet against his lower back as he carries me up the ramp to his ship.

"Take me home, Big Red."

"Take me home, Big Red."

EPILOGUE

ERIN

A MONTH LATER...

Pirate life is much easier than I thought it'd be, I think to myself. I twirl my new emerald necklace around my finger as I check on the plants in my hydroponic garden. The growth is slow for some of the vegetables, but since these aren't Earth veggies, I'm not sure if that's to be expected. Luckily, Khatazo carved out enough space in the food closet so they have room to grow.

The last month has flown by, and it's been the best month of my life. Once Qibor fully recovered from his procedure and got used to the feel of his new cybernetic arm, he started lining up jobs for us across Crinda. In the beginning, I didn't know how I'd be able to contribute to Khatazo's crew. They're a well-oiled machine when it comes to stealing from the rich, and I was worried I'd get in the way.

It turns out, this team has been lacking a key ingredient to their thievery: bait. I am spectacular bait. On our first job together, Aukellin told me to act dumb and look confused while wandering onto a slaver's ship orbiting Niifrahn, a planet not far from Huva II.

Khatazo immediately shot that idea down. "No, don't act dumb. Be yourself. Be Ehrn."

Once our ship locked onto theirs, I walked down the tunnel and played with the short hem of my skirt as I took in the unique, swirling lines on their ship's walls. The guards lowered their weapons immediately when I came into view, their tongues hanging out, and Khatazo, Aukellin, and Qibor charged past me, taking them down, as well as the rest of their crew.

We took the group of Niffrahnians we found locked in a large metal cage back to their home planet and kept the credits and jewels we found stashed in a closet for ourselves.

Our coffers are overflowing, and there are plenty of jobs ahead of us to keep us fat and happy as we map out our long-term plans.

"There you are," Khatazo growls as his fangs nip at my ear. Then he glides his tongue down my neck. "Mmm, you are my favorite meal."

"Oh yeah?" I reply, turning in his arms. I climb up my little stepladder, then sit on a ledge that Khatazo cleared to make room for my future plant babies. Lifting the hem of my dress, I part my thighs and expose my pussy. "Care for a snack then?"

I've come to learn there's no point in wearing underwear around him. We've had sex all over the ship, and my clit is in a perpetual state of throbbing need in his presence.

His pupils dilate as he devours me with his eyes, then lowers himself to his knees before me. I let my gaze drift over his body, feeling particularly grateful he walks around the ship shirtless all day, and I bite my lip as I follow the rigid planes of his chest. My mate is built like a weapon of mass destruction, but only I get to see the sweet jelly in the middle.

Once his mouth is on me, he doesn't go slow, because he's learned how much louder I scream when he goes fast, and like a typical guy, he loves hearing me shout his name. Khatazo's forked tongue delves between my folds and fills my core, marking it, claiming it, as his grip tightens on my thighs. I arch against his face, my clit seeking friction as I moan, "Yes, yes. More."

His tongue is hot as he thrusts in and out of me. My hands flail as they seek the edge of shelves, the wall, anything to hold on to as I roll my hips against his mouth. I feel his breath turn ragged as the tip of his nose brushes against my clit. He continues to lap at my dripping pussy, drinking me down as I wrap my hands around his tall horns and hold tight.

"Come for me," he mutters against my folds, the vibration of his voice bringing me closer to the edge.

In the same moment, his claws bite into the bare skin of my behind as his fangs brush along the side of my clit, and right there in the plant closet, I detonate. My eyes roll so far back, I worry they'll eject from my skull and bounce across the floor. My voice goes hoarse while screaming his name, and still, his tongue ripples inside the deepest corners of my body until my vision blurs.

I don't know how long my orgasm lasts. I just know that Khatazo's arms are wrapped around me, holding me firmly against his chest as I come down. Also, the front of his pants is soaking wet. I guess he came when I did.

I'm still shaking as he rubs my back and kisses along my collarbone.

"Mmm, you've got quite the tongue," I tell him, turning his face toward me so I can feel the fierce press of his lips.

He smiles against my mouth. "Not quite as talented as yours, but I appreciate the compliment."

This is certainly not what I imagined my future would look

like when I stepped off that shuttle on Huva II and strode toward the compound. It's not a quiet life, and maybe it's not always safe, but it's the only one I want. "We make a great team, huh?"

Khatazo chuckles, his bare chest rumbling against mine with the sound. "That we do, my heart. That we do."

BONUS EPILOGUE
QIBOR

"Qibor, what in the galactic *fiyk* are we doing here?" Ehrn asks as she strides onto the bridge, her hands on her waist and her expression angry as she looks at our approaching destination through the front window of our ship.

I grunt in response, indicating that I'm busy. We haven't even landed yet. Does she want us to crash into the port of Huva II? I must focus.

Ehrn looks to Khatazo impatiently, and my longtime friend clears his throat. "I didn't realize this was the plan. Why did you keep it from us?"

The answer should be obvious. If I told them this is where I'm meeting my contact to trade six *nymat* pearls for a new propellant tank, a blanket for Ehrn, and costumes for our next job, they would have refused to allow this meeting to take place. But these are things we need, and it was easier to let them think we were stopping at the station just north of Huva II to refuel.

"This trade is necessary. It's not up for discussion," I tell them, knowing Ehrn will not be satisfied with my usual silence.

Aukellin and Khatazo understand me in a way that she does not. Not yet, anyway. I don't have to explain my every decision to them. They either know what I'm thinking, or they trust me not to put them in harm's way.

Ehrn throws up her hands in annoyance, and I feel a twinge of guilt. She is part of our crew now, and I don't like seeing her upset, but this was a secret I had to keep. I don't expect the trade to take that long anyway. We will be in and out of Huva II without even a glimpse of the Cursed Compound.

Khatazo and his new mate sacrificed much of their sanity to make it to the finish line of Empress Motavvi's castle of nightmares, and the credits Khatazo earned here paid for my cybernetic arm. I owe him my life. The last thing I wish to do is uncover the trauma they are both still trying to work through.

As our ship lurches to a stop at our assigned slip, I get to my feet and stretch my arms above my head. I've gotten more comfortable using my replacement arm, but there are times when I swear I still feel the old one. The hand that was blown off somehow tingling in the dead of night. It's unsettling. "I shall be quick," I tell them, grabbing the small steel case containing the pearls and strapping it to my belt.

Behind me, I hear Aukellin emerge onto the bridge and ask why we're here. Khatazo tells him my plan, and then attempts to offer Ehrn some comfort. "We won't even leave the ship," he vows, his tone soft in a way that is only meant for her. "It will be like we were never here."

My contact is coming from a commuter shuttle, so I wander through the curved cobblestone streets until I find the landing zone for his shuttle. The screen above the slip indicates that the shuttle will arrive shortly.

With nothing to do but wait, I cross my arms over my chest and take in my surroundings.

This is a dreadful planet, ruled by the dreadfully corrupt

Empress Motavvi. Even the smell here has me wrinkling my nose. Huva II's main attraction is the compound, but there's also a small market with ten stalls offering food, drink, and compound-branded merchandise. That the empress deems it appropriate to sell clothing promoting a venue in which thousands die each turn of the sun speaks to the putrid lump of tissue inside her chest where a heart should be.

Growing impatient at the shuttle stop, I find myself wandering closer to the market, amused by the array of people here. There are so many different species filling these streets, at least half of which I can't identify. How strange that the quest for credits is the one thing we all have in common, not just in the Crinda Galaxy, but across several.

I'm so focused on looking at the people in front of me that I don't notice who is to my right until her short, slender frame slams into my side. She practically bounces off me, falling backward and landing with a pained grunt. I offer her my hand, but she doesn't take it. Her attire is...strange, and her face caked in colors that seem unnatural for her. Even her mane doesn't look like it belongs on her head.

She gets to her feet in a rush and tugs on the long orange strands of her mane, pulling it into place. What she does next leaves me stunned.

Her hands fly to her chest and form several shapes as her mouth moves. No sound emerges from her lips, but it's clear she's attempting to communicate with me. When her hands stop moving, she looks at me expectantly, but I'm not sure what to say. She repeats her hand gestures, slower this time, but I still don't know what they mean.

"Are you well?" I ask, not knowing what else to say. "Apologies if I hurt you. I didn't see you there."

Her hands start moving again, forming new shapes, and I focus my attention there, hoping this time, whatever she's trying to communicate will register in my mind. This is clearly a language I don't know, and I hate how helpless I feel.

"I don't know what you're saying," I tell her as my gaze drifts down her slight stature. She is small like Ehrn, and she has the same flat facial features. Though this female's skin is hidden behind the layers of odd paint, I notice her eyes are the same round shape as Ehrn's. Where Ehrn's are green, this female's are a rich shade of brown that I find myself studying closer than I probably should, given that I don't even know her name. Her shoulders are round and her hips are wide like Ehrn's too. Is she...human?

As soon as the question forms, confusion and fury follow close behind. What is she doing here? This place is not safe for her kind. Doesn't she know that? What could've brought such a delicate creature to such a wretched planet?

"Do you live here?" I ask. I don't expect an answer, but I want one nonetheless. "Where is home?" I make a sweeping gesture with my mechanical arm. "May I escort you there?"

She shakes her head, and I'm unsure if it's because she doesn't understand me or she is rejecting my offer.

We stand there, staring at each other, for several heartbeats, before she throws up her hands and starts walking away. My stomach forms a painful knot when I realize she's walking toward the compound.

Stop her, the voice in my head shouts. *By any means necessary.*

I race to catch up with her and gently grab hold of her arm. She whirls around and the blunt edges of her claws impale my eyes. Pain shoots through me as I stagger backward as I put a hand over my face. I try blinking the blurriness away, but my eyes sting so badly I worry I'm about to fall to my knees in this crowded little market.

It takes longer than I would like, but eventually, the pain

subsides, and I can detect shapes and colors once more. But once my vision clears, I don't see her anymore. The orange-maned human female has disappeared.

How did she slip away so quickly? Ehrn is fast, but not that fast.

Scanning the crowd, I look for a bright orange mane. I spot it bobbing up and down in the mass of people following the narrow paths toward the compound.

It's then that I abandon my plan to trade the pearls and come up with a new one in its place.

Fiyk this trade. This female needs protection, and I plan on giving it to her.

THANK you for reading ALLIANCE WITH THE ALIEN PIRATE! I hope you loved Erin and Khatazo's story. Are you wondering what happens when Qibor follows that mysterious human into the compound? Good news! You're about to find out!

RESCUED BY THE ALIEN PIRATE is coming soon!

ALSO FROM IVY

<u>ALIENS OF OLUURA</u>

Saving His Mate

Charming His Mate

Stealing His Mate

Keeping His Mate

Healing His Mate

Enchanting Her Mate

(This series isn't finished. There's plenty more to come!)

<u>STRANDED ON EARTH</u>

Her Alien Bodyguard

Her Alien Neighbor

Her Alien Librarian

Her Alien Student

Her Alien Boss

ENJOY THIS BOOK?

Did you enjoy this book? If so, please leave a review! It helps others find my work.

Get all the deets on new releases, bonus chapters, teasers, and giveaways by signing up for my <u>newsletter</u>.

RESOURCES

National Domestic Violence Hotline
1.800.799.SAFE (7233)
thehotline.org

SAMHSA (Substance Abuse and Mental Health Services
Administration Hotline)
1-800-662-HELP (4357)
TTY: 1-800-487-4889
samhsa.gov

RAINN (Rape, Abuse, & Incest National Network)
1-800-656-4673 (call or chat)
rainn.org

National Suicide Prevention Hotline
1-800-273-8255 (call or chat)
suicideprevention.org

About the Author

Ivy Knox has always been a voracious reader of romance novels, but quickly found her home in sci-fi romance because life on Earth can be kind of a drag. When she's not lost on faraway worlds created by her favorite authors, she's creating her own.

Ivy lives with her husband and two neurotic (but very cute) dogs in the Midwest. When she's not reading or writing, she's probably watching *Superstore*, *Bridgerton*, *The Fall of the House of Usher*, or *What We Do in the Shadows* for the millionth time.